Sharon Apple

THE BOBBSEY TWINS
AND THE
TALKING FOX MYSTERY

"Drop me!" says the stuffed fox to the jewel thief, as Bert and Nan Bobbsey are chasing him while Freddie and Flossie have gone for the police. This is only one of the Bobbsey Twins' many adventures in Quebec. They find themselves with Alphonse, a homeless St. Bernard puppy. Fun and adventures follow as they try to give him away only to have him turn up again. In the end, the children solve a baffling mystery, making several people happy, and restore Alphonse and the talking fox to their rightful owners.

THE BOBBSEY TWINS
By Laura Lee Hope

"Wait! I see a light!" Freddie called.

The
Bobbsey Twins
and the
Talking Fox
Mystery

By

LAURA LEE HOPE

GROSSET & DUNLAP

A NATIONAL GENERAL COMPANY

Publishers   *New York*

PRINTED IN THE UNITED STATES OF AMERICA
LIBRARY OF CONGRESS CATALOG CARD NO. 79–106307
The Bobbsey Twins and the Talking Fox Mystery

CONTENTS

THE BOBBSEY TWINS
AND THE
TALKING FOX MYSTERY

CHAPTER I

THE FOUR-LEGGED THIEF

"HURRAH! We're going to see the talking fox!" Flossie Bobbsey exclaimed.

"Foxes can't talk," Freddie declared.

The two blond, blue-eyed twins, six years old, were on their way to a friend's home in Canada with their mother and twin brother and sister, Bert and Nan. They were twelve. Mrs. Bobbsey was driving the family station wagon.

"You'll see," Bert told Freddie. Bert had dark hair and eyes like his twin, Nan. "Just ask the fox any question you want, and you'll get an answer."

Nan laughed. *This* she wanted to see.

"I believe," said Mrs. Bobbsey, "there's another mystery connected with the talking fox."

"Oh goody!" Flossie exclaimed, clapping her hands. "What is it?"

"I don't know," her mother replied. "But I'm sure Monsieur Valjean will tell us when we reach his place."

Flossie asked, "Is Muss-Yuh his first name?"

Mrs. Bobbsey and the older twins laughed. "No, dear. That means mister in French. They often write it capital M with a period after it," said Nan.

Her mother added, "Where we're going, near Quebec, most people speak French. Better practice the word, Flossie."

As Flossie repeated it over to herself, Bert and Freddie said they were hungry. Their mother nodded and soon pulled into a field near a stream with shade trees. Everyone got out.

Flossie and Freddie each carried a paper box tied with string. Inside were sandwiches and cup cakes. Bert and Nan brought cold drinks in jugs and ice cream.

"Oh, look!" Flossie cried out.

A huge St. Bernard puppy was bounding toward them. Without warning he grabbed the end of Flossie's box between his teeth and shook it hard. The string came off. The box opened and sandwiches flew in all directions.

"Oh!" cried Mrs. Bobbsey. "Stop that!"

As the dog grabbed a roast beef sandwich, the Bobbseys heard a whistle. Then a girl's voice called, "Alphonse! Come here!" She clapped her hands and whistled again.

The dog dropped the bread, gulped down the meat, then bounded across the field. The Bobbseys could not see anyone, but in a moment a car

Sandwiches flew in all directions.

roared away and they guessed the pup had returned to his owner.

"Naughty, naughty Alphonse!" Flossie scolded as she looked at a peanut butter and jelly sandwich on the ground. The wrapping had come off, and already ants were crawling over it.

Fortunately nothing else had been ruined, and the Bobbseys ate every scrap of food. Several bees tried to share the picnic but the twins shooed them away.

Within an hour the Bobbseys were on their way again. As the miles slid by, the children looked out the windows at the broad blue river which ran beside the road.

After a while Freddie pulled a small rubber mouse from his pocket and began squeaking it. "Here comes Mousie!" he exclaimed and ran the toy over the back of Nan's neck.

"Stop it!" she exclaimed. "That thing squeaks just like a real mouse! It gives me the shivers."

Freddie giggled. "All girls are scared of mice!"

As he spoke, Mrs. Bobbsey pulled into a driveway lined with big maple trees.

"Here we are," she said and parked. "Do you see anything odd about this house?"

The children looked curiously at the large, gray frame building with a steeply sloping roof.

A porch ran across the entire front of the house.

"There's a sign next to the door!" said Flossie. "It has an Indian painted on it!"

"And the words, *The Talking Fox,*" added Bert.

As they stepped from the car, Mrs. Bobbsey explained that the house had been an inn for years before M. Valjean had bought it. "All old inns had names," she added.

She rang the bell, and a few moments later the door was opened by a short, stout man with pink cheeks and dark curly hair.

"Madame Bobbsey!" he cried. "Come in, come in! How glad I am to see all of you!"

His black eyes sparkled with pleasure as he drew the family into a cozy hall with a bright blue rug on the floor. At one side a staircase led to the second floor.

Mrs. Bobbsey introduced her children. With a delightful French accent, the host repeated the twins' names and made a little bow to each one.

Freddie had spotted a stuffed gray fox on a little table near the door. "Is this the talking fox?" he asked eagerly.

M. Valjean started to reply, but just then the telephone rang. Excusing himself, he hurried behind a tall counter-like desk beside the staircase to answer it.

The twins clustered around the stuffed animal. Flossie petted the soft fur with one finger.

"He's so nice," she said. "See what bright little button eyes he has!"

"He's pretty old, I think," Nan remarked. "His fur is a little moth-eaten."

"Let's give him a name," said Freddie.

"I know!" exclaimed Flossie. "We'll call him Mooseer Foxy!"

"*Muss-yuh,* Flossie," said Nan with a smile.

"Hello, Monsieur Foxy," said Freddie. "Please talk to us."

At that moment they heard cries from the open door at the end of the hall. A large St. Bernard puppy ran out with a cabbage in his mouth. After him raced four people shouting in French. One was a small, thin man with a large black mustache. Behind him was a stout, dark-haired woman in a white apron. Next came a pretty, teenage girl in a red dress, followed by a boy of about ten.

"Nice doggie!" said Flossie, stepping toward the puppy. "Give me the cabbage!"

The dog gave a joyful bark and leaped on the little girl. As she sat down hard, the cabbage rolled across the floor.

"*Non,* Alphonse, *non!*" cried the girl in red.

It was the same dog who had stolen the picnic sandwich!

M. Valjean hung up the telephone and rushed to help Flossie. But the small man and Mrs. Bobbsey had already lifted the child to her feet. The large woman put an arm around Flossie and spoke rapidly in French.

"My mother wants to know if you are hurt," said the little boy. He spoke with a French accent. "My sister and I speak English," he explained, "but *Maman* and *Papa* do not."

"I'm all right," said Flossie breathlessly. Meanwhile Freddie picked up the cabbage and gave it to the man with the mustache.

M. Valjean introduced the woman as his sister, Madame Marie Leclerc. The little man was her husband, Charles, a chef. "He runs a catering business from our kitchen. We all live here together," M. Valjean said.

"You should see the cakes Papa makes!" exclaimed the little boy, rolling his eyes.

"My name is Lisette," said the daughter, smiling. She had big dark eyes and long, shiny black hair. "This is Louis."

A wide impish smile lit up the boy's thin face. "I will practice on you my English," he said. "You will be here two weeks, no?"

"Yes," said Nan, smiling. "Then my father will pick us up." She explained that Mr. Bobbsey had driven the family as far as Montreal.

"Then he flew to Ontario on business," Bert added.

"Daddy has a lumber company in Lakeport,"

Nan said. Then she introduced the children.

"We have two dogs," Flossie spoke up. "Spot and Waggo."

"This is Alphonse," Louis said, putting a hand on the puppy's collar.

"We know," said Nan with a smile. "We've met him before." She explained about the picnic lunch.

Lisette apologized for the dog. She explained that he had been given to them by a Monsieur Durand. "My father catered a large party for him, and then the man couldn't pay Papa. One morning three weeks ago, we found Alphonse tied to our front porch with a note on his collar. Monsieur Durand left him here in payment of his bill."

"The dog is very lovable," M. Valjean said, "but he has two bad habits. He eats too much and is always in trouble."

"Maman, Papa and Uncle Henri want to get rid of him," said Lisette.

"Can't you send him back to Monsieur Durand?" asked Bert.

"Nobody knows where he is," replied the girl. "He disappeared about two months ago, owing everybody money."

"Alphonse is only one problem," said M. Valjean, taking a bunch of keys from a hook on the wall behind the desk. "We have a mystery here."

He turned to Mrs. Bobbsey. "When your husband and I arranged this visit on the telephone I mentioned it." His jolly face grew puzzled. "He said that was fine, because the twins were detectives."

"Are they?" asked Louis, wide-eyed.

Mrs. Bobbsey explained that her children had solved a number of puzzling cases.

"What is your mystery, Monsieur Valjean?" Bert put in eagerly.

Before he could answer, two men in gray suits came down the stairs.

M. Valjean introduced the first one as M. Noir. He had dark hair. The other, with blond hair, was named Verde.

The Bobbseys greeted them pleasantly. The men nodded coldly and went out the front door.

"The *moosoors* are not very friendly," Flossie thought.

M. Valjean explained that the two had arrived an hour before. "They walked right in and asked for a room. I told them that this house was not an inn any more. One of the men nearly fainted."

Lisette added, "They said they were sick and needed a few quiet days in the country." She smiled. "And Uncle Henri is so soft-hearted, he let them stay."

The stout man's face grew pinker. "What could I do? Certainly they both look sick and pale. And they are paying something. Now," he said cheerfully, "Charles and I will get your bags, and Lisette will show you to your rooms."

Lisette and Louis led the visitors to the second floor. The girl gave them three rooms in a row. All had big double beds with gaily embroidered spreads. There were starched white curtains at the windows.

"You boys will be in the first one with Louis," said Lisette.

"I'll sleep on the cot," her brother added cheerfully.

"Nan and Flossie have my room," said Lisette, smiling. "I moved up to the attic. Madame Bobbsey is next to the girls."

"There are a lot of rooms in this house," remarked Nan, looking at the doors on both sides of the long corridor.

"How come the inn was called *The Talking Fox?*" Freddie asked.

"It was named for an Indian chief who used to live around here long ago," said Louis. "That's a painting of him on the sign next to the front door."

After the twins had washed their faces and hands, Louis took them down to the porch.

"Tell us about the mystery," said Bert eagerly.

Louis looked scared. "All this week we've been hearing noises at night," he said softly, "like somebody trying to force open a window or a door. And then last night something awful happened!"

"What?" Nan asked.

"Uncle Henri and I heard noises. We came downstairs to investigate. And in the moonlight we saw a one-eyed man looking in the parlor window." Louis shivered. "I think it was Old One-Eye's ghost!"

"Who's he?" asked Freddie.

"A hundred years ago there was a gang of smugglers who stayed in the inn," said Louis. "The leader was called Old One-Eye, because he had only one eye. He was a terrible man! Maybe he's trying to come back."

"That can't be," said Bert. "You don't believe in spooks, do you?"

"Not exactly," said the boy uncertainly. "But it was a very scary face."

"Don't be frightened," said Freddie. "We'll catch the bad man for you."

That night when the twins settled down in their soft beds, they were too excited about the new mystery to sleep. Lying awake, the girls heard a board creak loudly outside their door.

"Maybe it's Old One-Eye sneaking around," Flossie whispered.

Nan got up, put on her robe and slippers, then hurried to the door.

"Wait for me," said Flossie, catching her sleeve. The girls peered into the dimly lit hall. It was empty.

Just then the boys' door opened and Bert and Freddie stepped out. Freddie was holding his toy mouse.

"You heard it too?" asked Bert softly. As Nan nodded they all tiptoed to the head of the stairs and looked down.

A figure in a bathrobe was going stealthily down the steps. A shaft of moonlight from a window showed it to be the dark-haired guest, M. Noir.

"What's he doing?" whispered Freddie. In his excitement he squeezed the rubber mouse. There was a loud *squeak!*

CHAPTER II

THE SLEEPWALKER

WHEN the toy squeaked, the man on the stairs froze.

"Don't be afraid, Monsieur Noir," Nan called down to him. "It was just Freddie's rubber mouse."

M. Noir did not answer. Instead, he turned around and began to walk stiffly up the stairs. His arms were straight out in front of him and his eyes were wide open. He walked right past the children without looking at them or speaking.

"What's the matter with him?" whispered Flossie.

"He's sleepwalking, I guess," said Bert softly.

The twins watched as M. Noir went to his room at the end of the hall.

"That was creepy," said Freddie with a shiver. "Why didn't we wake him up?"

"It's better not to," said Nan. "You might scare him. The best thing is to lead a sleepwalker back to his bed where he'll be safe."

"Anyhow, I'm glad it wasn't Old One-Eye," said Flossie as the twins went to their rooms.

In the morning, breakfast was served in a big, sunny dining room off the first floor hall. The guests sat at a large round table with the Canadians. Mme. Leclerc served tasty omelette and slices of Canadian bacon.

Everyone talked cheerfully except the two men. Suddenly M. Verde spoke up.

"I want to tell all of you something," he said in good English. "My friend is a sleepwalker. If any of you should see him walking around at night, do not be alarmed."

While Lisette translated for her parents, the two men went on eating and said no more. When they had finished breakfast, they excused themselves and left the dining room.

M. Valjean sighed. "They are rather strange men," he said. "I'm beginning to be sorry I let them stay."

"Don't worry, Uncle Henri," said Lisette. "They're planning to remain only a few days."

"Did anybody hear strange noises last night?"

The twins told about having seen M. Noir.

"I meant sounds like Old One-Eye trying to get in," said Louis.

No one had seen or heard any sign of the would-be intruder.

"Maybe he has given up," said M. Valjean. "I hope so."

When breakfast was over, Mrs. Bobbsey insisted upon washing the dishes. Nan and Flossie offered to dry them. Mme. Leclerc smiled and patted the girls' heads as she gave them dish towels. Then she and Lisette went upstairs to make beds.

Meanwhile the boys watched M. Leclerc work at the kitchen table. He was frosting dozens of little cakes with chocolate from a big bowl. Now and then he stirred the creamy icing with a wooden spoon. Later the cakes would be put in the freezer.

"What are all these for?" Bert asked.

"We're having a big party a week from now," replied Louis. "It's for a birthday."

"Whose?" asked Nan.

"This house," said Louis with a grin. He explained that the former inn would be two hundred years old. "We've invited all our friends to come and celebrate."

"Oh, goody!" exclaimed Flossie. "We love parties!"

At that moment Alphonse trotted into the kitchen, his big bushy tail wagging. He jumped onto a chair beside the table and sniffed at the cakes.

"*Non,* Alphonse!" cried Louis as his father let out a sharp cry of alarm.

Startled, the dog whirled. As he leaped down, his tail knocked the bowl to the floor. It broke, spattering chocolate in all directions.

Angrily M. Leclerc picked up the gooey

spoon and hurled it after the fleeing dog. A blob of chocolate flew off and hit Freddie on the nose —SPLAT!

The little boy looked surprised and then everyone laughed—except Louis' father. He ran over and put an arm around Freddie and spoke soothingly in French.

"I'm all right," said Freddie, giggling. He wiped the chocolate off his nose with a paper towel.

To make up for the accident, the chef gave each twin a frosted cake. They in turn helped clean up the mess on the floor.

Shaking his head, Louis' father spoke grimly in French. The boy translated.

"Papa says somebody must keep an eye on Alphonse so he does not come back into the kitchen."

"I'll do it," Nan offered.

"You children go find the dog," said Mrs. Bobbsey, taking Nan's towel. "He ran out the back screen door. It wasn't closed tightly."

The girls followed the boys into the back yard. Alphonse was lying beside the stoop with his head between his paws.

"Let's take him for a walk," said Flossie.

Nan looked toward some woods at the rear of the big yard. "How about in there?" she suggested.

"Not me," said Bert. "See you later." He went off around the side of the house.

"Where are you going?" Freddie called. But his brother did not answer. The little boy looked disappointed. He liked to go places with his older brother.

"Don't worry," said Nan. "We'll have fun without him. Maybe he's building something or has found a special place to fish. Where's Alphonse's leash?" she asked Louis.

"Here." He took it from a hook on the wall beside the door, and Nan attached the leather lead to the dog's collar.

"I don't want to go for a walk," said Freddie. There was something else he was eager to do.

"Then you and I will stay here," said Louis.

The girls started off with the dog. They passed an old stable and disappeared among the trees.

"Louis," said Freddie, "did you ever hear the fox talk?"

"You mean that one in our front hall?" Louis started to laugh. "But no!"

Before he could say more, his mother called him.

"I have to go now," said Louis. "I'll see you later."

As the older boy ran into the kitchen, Freddie hurried around to the front of the house. He went up on the porch and, finding the screen door unlocked, stepped into the hall. There was no one in sight. He walked over to the fox and stroked the gray fur.

The fox was talking!

"Hello, Freddie!" said a squeaky voice.

The fox was talking!

Freddie's heart started to pound. He was sure a stuffed fox could not really talk! He looked around, but the hall was empty.

"Who are you looking for?" asked the voice.

"I—I don't know," said Freddie, confused. "I thought maybe there was a record player somewhere."

"Don't be silly," said the voice. "A record player couldn't say your name or see what you're doing."

"That's right," whispered Freddie.

"Don't be afraid," said the voice kindly. "You ought to be proud. I don't talk to everybody— just to special people."

Freddie gulped. "Will you talk to Bert and Nan and Flossie, too?"

"I'll see," said the fox. "Now run along."

Bursting with amazement, Freddie went through the house looking for someone to tell. He found only Mme. and M. Leclerc working hard in the kitchen.

"No use telling them," thought Freddie. "They don't understand English."

The little boy went into the back yard where there was a big maple tree with a swing hanging from a branch. He played on it for a while. Then he explored the stable, but decided this was no fun without horses. Near noon Bert strolled into the yard, and Freddie explained about the fox.

His brother grinned. "I told you he'd talk," Bert said. "Here come Nan and Flossie with Alphonse. Tell them."

The little boy poured out his story to the girls and also to Louis.

Nan laughed. "Come on, Freddie," she said. "We all know foxes can't talk."

"Honest, Nan, he did!" Freddie said.

"Louis," said Nan eagerly, "there's a big pond back in the woods. May we go swimming there?"

"But of course," he replied. "We always do."

At that moment Mme. Leclerc called them to lunch. Mrs. Bobbsey, Lisette and M. Valjean had returned from a shopping trip into the village. Freddie told them about the fox, but his mother and Nan treated it as a joke. The others grinned and remained silent.

Later M. Leclerc invited everyone to the kitchen to see the finished cakes. M. Verde and M. Noir excused themselves and went upstairs. Everyone else trooped to the kitchen where three large trays of fancy cakes were arranged on the kitchen table.

"Oh, they're bee-yoo-ti-ful!" said Flossie.

The chef beamed and his mustache twitched proudly as everyone praised his work. He bowed modestly, then said something to his wife and left the room.

"Now Papa will take his afternoon nap," said Lisette. "He asked my mother to put the cakes in the freezer. I'll wash the dishes."

"I'll help you," Nan offered.

Just then the telephone rang and M. Valjean hurried away to answer it. In a few moments he called his sister to come and talk. As she hurried off, Mme. Leclerc spoke over her shoulder to her daughter.

"Oui, maman," said the girl. "I have to put the cakes away as soon as we finish," she told Nan.

"Come on, Louis," said Freddie, "I've got an idea."

The two boys went out the back door with Flossie tagging after them. Mrs. Bobbsey had already gone upstairs.

"Lisette," said Bert, "I'd like to ask some questions about the mystery."

Her dark eyes grew wide. "I know very little," she said, "but I will tell you one thing. Uncle Henri is not a man to imagine things. If he says he saw a one-eyed face at the window, you can be sure he did."

Soon the dishes were in the cupboard. "Now to put the cakes away!" said Lisette. Before she could turn toward the table, loud yells for help came from outside the house.

"That's Freddie!" exclaimed Nan.

"And Louis!" said Bert.

As he dashed into the yard with the two girls

behind him, Freddie appeared in the stable door.

"Come quick!" he cried and ran inside again.

The three raced across the grass and into the gloomy old building. They could hear Flossie crying, but she was nowhere in sight! Freddie and Louis were at the far end of the stable, stooping over to look down at something.

"It's Flossie!" cried Freddie. "She fell through the floor!"

CHAPTER III

GOOD-BY TO ALPHONSE

THE older twins and Lisette ran past the empty horse stalls to where the two boys were kneeling by the hole in the floor.

"Flossie!" cried Nan, looking down into the gloomy pit. "Are you hurt?"

"I don't know," sobbed the little girl. Next to her was a large round-topped trunk.

Bert lowered himself into the hole and lifted his sister out of it. Nan and Lisette looked her over carefully.

"You're okay, Flossie," said Nan, drying the little girl's tears.

"What happened?" Lisette asked.

"We were detecting," said Freddie. "I thought maybe we'd fine some signs of Old One-Eye out here. We moved that big trunk away from the wall to look for clues behind it."

"I guess the floor was rotten," Louis put in. "The trunk went right through and Flossie went with it."

"I'm not surprised," said Lisette. "This tack

23

room is the oldest part of the stable. It used to be a little house. That's how it happens to have a wooden floor with a space under it."

"Where are your horses?" Nan asked.

"We've never had any," said Louis. "We just keep barrels and garden tools in here."

"Is there a flashlight in the stable?" Bert called. "This old chest has some things in it."

Louis took a battery lantern from a shelf. As he shone it into the hole, Bert handed up an old fiddle and a bow.

Freddie gave a whoop of joy. "Oh, let me try it!" He took the instrument and drew the bow across the dry strings. A loud squawking sound followed.

The next moment there was a deafening screech and a large dark shape swooped down from the rafters at them.

"Watch out!" cried Lisette.

As they ducked, a big owl skimmed over their heads and out the door.

Bert chuckled. "I guess he didn't like Freddie's playing."

"Never mind," said Lisette, patting the little boy's shoulder. "I'll teach him to play a tune on the fiddle."

"Good," said Freddie happily.

"Here are a lot of old-fashioned clothes," said Bert. He began handing up long skirts, shawls and bonnets.

"Let's take them outside where we can see

better," Lisette suggested. In a few minutes everything was under the big tree.

"Maybe we could dress up in these old clothes for the party," said Nan eagerly, trying on a bonnet.

"That's a good idea," Lisette agreed.

Suddenly Bert noticed Alphonse lying beside the swing. He had not leaped up to greet the children as usual.

"What's the matter with him?" Bert asked. "He looks sort of funny."

Nan kneeled beside the dog. "I think he's sick," she said. "His nose is hot."

"Maybe he ate something he shouldn't have," said Flossie.

As Nan peered closer, she got a whiff of chocolate. She gasped. "The cakes!"

"Oh, no!" Lisette cried, turning pale.

The girls raced for the house with the others after them. Bursting into the kitchen, Nan gave a cry of dismay. Most of the little cakes were gone! The others had been mashed or broken.

"What's the matter?" asked M. Valjean, hurrying in from the hall. Seeing the ruined food, he groaned and went to tell his sister.

Within minutes the kitchen was full of excited grownups. Mrs. Bobbsey came running from upstairs. Mme. Leclerc wrung her hands as her husband strode up and down, holding his head.

"I'm sorry," said Nan, beginning to cry. "It's

all my fault. I was supposed to watch Alphonse!"

"And I was supposed to put the cakes away," said Lisette, weeping.

Mme. Leclerc insisted she should have put the cakes away herself. Suddenly M. Leclerc shouted and signaled for silence. He made a short, firm speech. Louis translated.

"Papa says *he* should have put the cakes away himself," he announced. "The girls are not to blame."

"No," put in M. Valjean, "it is the dog's fault. But never again will he make trouble in this house! I have found another home for him."

"Where?" asked Louis.

"With Monsieur Girard."

Lisette looked shocked. "Not Monsieur Girard!"

"He's mean!" exclaimed Louis.

His sister told the twins that the man lived a short distance up the road. "He never talks to anybody. All he cares about is his car. He's always polishing it."

"Once I saw him kick a cat out of his flower bed," added Louis.

"It can't be helped," said M. Valjean unhappily. "The matter is settled."

He explained that the telephone call after lunch had been from M. Girard. The man had heard that the family wanted to find a home for the dog. He needed a watchdog and had offered to take Alphonse. "The animal goes tonight," finished M. Valjean.

As the others sadly cleaned away the ruined cakes, Bert told M. Valjean about the broken stable floor.

He looked worried. "I'm glad no one was hurt. I'll have to hire a man to get the trunk out of there and fix the hole."

"I had almost forgotten those old things," he added. "They belonged to my grandparents."

"Moosoor Valjean," said Flossie, "may we wear the costumes for the party?"

"But, yes! A good idea!" he said, smiling.

"Flossie," Nan remarked quietly, "you said it wrong again."

The little girl sighed. *"Monsir*—is that right?"

As Nan shook her head, M. Valjean chuckled. "Why don't all of you children call me Uncle Henri? I would like that."

"I would too," said Flossie happily. "It's more friendly." The others looked pleased at the idea.

"Bring the clothes to my room," said Mrs. Bobbsey. "I'll alter them to fit you."

"And I'll play the fiddle at the party," Freddie spoke up eagerly. "Lisette's going to teach me."

That evening Alphonse felt a little better, but not well enough to walk to M. Girard's house.

Mrs. Bobbsey volunteered to drive him there.

The girls led the big pup out to the station wagon. He sat down in the drive, his head drooping.

"He usually loves to go for a ride," said Lisette.

Bert and Louis lifted him onto the back seat. "Wow! He's heavy!" Bert remarked.

"No wonder," said Freddie. "He's full of chocolate cake."

The twins and Louis piled into the car. Lisette stayed behind and waved as they drove away.

In a few minutes Louis pointed to a small, neat white house beside the road. "That's it," he said. "There's Monsieur Girard now."

A thin, sharp-faced man in a blue shirt was watering a bed of petunias beside the drive. Mrs. Bobbsey pulled in behind a small, shiny black car.

Louis spoke to the man in French, and he replied shortly. His hard black eyes flicked over the dog and he spoke again sourly.

"We have to tie Alphonse in the garage," Louis translated. The boys lifted the dog out of the car.

Slowly the children walked him to the back of the house and put him in the garage. Bert fastened his leash to the door handle.

"Is Alphonse going to live in here?" asked Nan.

"Yes," said Louis gloomily.

"But there's no bed for him," said Nan, worried.

"That's not the worst," Louis replied. "Monsieur Girard says he is going to feed him very small meals because Alphonse is too fat."

"Oh, poor doggie!" exclaimed Flossie. She put her arms around his furry neck and gave him a hug. Sadly, the other children said good-by, too. As they walked away, Alphonse whimpered.

By the time they were back in the car, tears were rolling down Flossie's cheeks.

"I think we all need to cheer up," said Mrs. Bobbsey. "Maybe a little ice cream will make us feel better."

In a short time she pulled up before a small sweetshop on the main street. The children enjoyed their ice cream, but they could not help thinking how their pet would have loved it.

When they reached M. Valjean's house, gay music was coming from the parlor. Nan peered into the cheerful room with its heavy, old-fashioned furniture. Lisette was playing the piano.

"Come in," she called cheerfully. "I'll teach you a song for the party."

Mrs. Bobbsey went upstairs. The twins and Louis gathered around the piano. Lisette sang in a clear, strong voice and the children's feet began tapping. Patiently Lisette taught them the French words and the tune. Soon they were singing along with her.

Finally, laughing, she said, "That's enough for now. Tomorrow I will get new strings for the fiddle and give Freddie his first lesson."

The children went to bed early. Near midnight the boys were awakened by someone shaking them. It was Louis.

"I'm hungry," he said. "You want some cookies and milk?"

"That sounds great," said Bert. Freddie was already putting on his bathrobe and slippers.

The three tiptoed downstairs, through the moonlit hall and into the kitchen. Louis closed the door softly and turned on the light. While Bert took milk from the refrigerator, Louis went to the pantry for a stone crock.

"Help yourselves," he said. The boys dug in and took out big, soft molasses cookies.

"Umm, good," murmured Freddie as he bit into one.

Louis looked sad as he drank his milk. "Poor Alphonse!"

"He's sleeping on that hard garage floor." Freddie sighed.

Bert's thoughts were on the mystery. "The fellow who has been trying to break in here didn't come last night," he said. "I wonder if he'll show up tonight."

"I hope not," said Louis. "I'd be scared to see that mean old one-eyed face again."

"Me too," said Freddie.

After the boys finished eating, they tidied the

Someone was shaking Bert and Freddie.

kitchen. Louis turned out the light and reached for the doorknob. At that moment there was a loud creaking noise from the hall.

"Somebody's out there!" whispered Bert.

Freddie gulped. "Maybe it's Old One-Eye!"

CHAPTER IV

DISTURBING NEWS

QUIETLY Bert opened the kitchen door. M. Noir was tiptoeing across the floor in his robe and slippers. He stopped at the little table and picked up the fox.

"He's sleepwalking again," said Freddie.

The man stiffened but did not turn in their direction.

"We'd better take him upstairs," said Bert. "He might hurt himself wandering around the house like this."

The three boys walked over to the man. Gently Bert took the fox from his hands and put it back on the table.

While the Bobbseys guided him up the staircase, Louis ran ahead and knocked on M. Noir's room door. It opened and M. Verde, wearing pajamas, looked out in amazement.

"We found your friend downstairs," said Bert. "He was sleepwalking again."

For a moment M. Verde seemed unable to

"We found your friend sleepwalking," said Bert.

speak. Then he whispered, "Thank you." He pulled the other man into the room and shut the door.

"I wonder why he went to the fox," said Bert. "Maybe he was dreaming about it."

"Listen, fellows," said Freddie earnestly, "that fox talks. I heard him."

Bert smiled and put his hand on his brother's shoulder. "I believe anything you say, Freddie."

Louis grinned. "Me, too! But this I must hear myself."

Just then a door opened down the hall and Mme. Leclerc, her hair in a long, fat braid, looked out. She spoke sternly to Louis in French.

"We'd better get back to bed," he said. "And no more talking." As Louis' mother watched from her doorway, the boys scooted into their room.

At breakfast next morning neither of the two men appeared. Bert told the others about the sleepwalker.

Uncle Henri frowned. "I don't like the idea of his wandering around here at night."

"At least it's not Old One-Eye," said Freddie, pouring maple syrup on his pancakes.

"Apparently the intruder hasn't been around for two nights," said Mrs. Bobbsey.

"It is odd," said Bert thoughtfully. "The person must have wanted very much to break into the house. After all, he tried night after night for a whole week. Now he has suddenly given up."

"Maybe he hasn't," said Nan uneasily. "He might be trying to get in some other way."

They heard the telephone ring. Uncle Henri excused himself to answer it. In a few minutes he was back and his face was grim.

"That was M. Girard," he announced. "He says he will not keep Alphonse any longer. We have to come for him at once."

"What happened?" Nan asked.

Uncle Henri shrugged. "Girard was so angry he could hardly talk."

Quickly Louis translated for his parents. M. Leclerc rolled his eyes and struck his brow. His wife sighed and shook her head.

"I am busy," said Uncle Henri firmly. "Someone else will have to go for the dog."

Immediately after breakfast, the chef hurried to the kitchen to bake new cakes. Lisette went upstairs with her mother.

"I want to begin on the costumes," said Mrs. Bobbsey. "You children can call for Alphonse."

Louis and the twins started down the road at once, wondering what kind of trouble the dog was in now. As they neared M. Girard's house, they saw the man's small black car in the driveway.

"Look!" cried Bert, bursting into laughter. "Alphonse is behind the wheel!"

But as the children ran into the driveway, their smiles vanished. M. Girard was standing beside the car dressed in a black suit and hat looking as if he were going to the city. He was speaking angrily to Alphonse and cuffing the dog with his gloves.

"Stop! Don't do that!" cried Nan. "You'll hurt him!"

As the man stepped back, the twins saw that one of Alphonse's front legs was wedged between the spokes of the steering wheel.

"He can't get out," said Bert. "We'll have to help him."

"How did it happen?" asked Flossie.

Louis questioned M. Girard, who replied furiously. Trying not to laugh, Louis told the Bobbseys what he had said.

During the night Alphonse had chewed through his leash. In the morning when M. Girard came out and opened his car door, the dog ran over and jumped in. The man tried to drag the big St. Bernard out and in the struggle Alphonse got tangled in the wheel.

"I'm littlest," said Flossie. "I'll crawl underneath and push his leg up."

"Good," said Bert, "and then we'll lift him out."

M. Girard spoke sharply and pointed to the flower bed beside the drive.

"Watch out for the flowers," said Louis. "M.

Girard will blow off his lid if we step on one."

"Blow his top, you mean," said Bert, grinning.

Louis laughed. "I need more practice with my American slang," he said.

Meanwhile Flossie had crept into the car under the steering wheel. Carefully she pushed the dog's shaggy leg up between the spokes.

"Okay, now," said Bert. "Here you go, Alphonse."

As he and Nan lifted the heavy dog out, the animal struggled. Caught off balance, the twins staggered backward.

"Be careful!" cried Flossie. "The flowers!" But the twins fell into the petunia bed with Alphonse on top of them.

As M. Girard shouted with rage, the younger children broke into giggles. The other two got to their feet and quickly guided the dog out of the crushed petunias.

"We're very sorry," said Nan.

"We really couldn't help it," added Bert.

But M. Girard drowned them out with angry French and pointed toward the road. Leading Alphonse by his broken leash, the children hurried away. The dog trotted briskly beside them.

"At least he's not sick any more," said Nan.

"No, but I don't think M. Girard feels so good," said Bert.

Nan nodded. "He's a mean man, but you really can't blame him for being angry about his flowers. I think we ought to give him new ones to replace the ones we mashed." The other children agreed.

"Maman has a petunia bed in the side yard," said Louis. "She will give us some, I'm sure."

When they reached the house, Bert and Freddie took Alphonse to the back yard and tied him to the big tree with a piece of clothesline. Meanwhile Louis and the girls went inside to ask Mme. Leclerc about the flowers.

They came out a few minutes later with a large cardboard box and two trowels. Carefully Nan and Bert dug up some petunias and placed them in the box. Then, taking the trowels, they all trooped back up the road again to M. Girard's house. The black car was gone.

"He's not home," said Bert.

"I'm glad," said Freddie, " 'cause he was awful mad at us."

Working quickly, the older twins dug up the ruined flowers. Then everyone helped to plant fresh ones where the others had been.

When everything was tidy, Louis took a pencil from his pocket and wrote a note on a small piece of paper, saying again that they were sorry. He stuck it under the front door. Then the children walked back to *The Talking Fox*.

Freddie stopped at the front porch. "I'm going in and see if Monsieur Foxy will talk to me again. Why don't the rest of you come, too?"

Bert grinned. "You get him to talk first, then

call me. See you later," he added and went into the house.

Freddie turned to the others. "Come on! Maybe Monsieur Foxy will talk to all of us."

Louis grinned. "You said he only spoke to special people. He probably won't do it for us."

"Let's play on the swing," said Nan.

"All right," Louis agreed. "Come on!" He led the girls around the corner of the house.

For a few minutes Freddie sat alone on the steps, frowning. He knew a stuffed animal really should not be able to talk, and yet he had heard the fox speaking! It was a puzzle!

The little boy got up and went into the front hall to have another look at the mysterious creature. M. Verde was there, feeling around the animal's neck. The man glanced up, startled.

"Hello," said Freddie. "It's fun to pet the fox, isn't it?" He walked over to the stuffed animal. "I like to do it, too."

M. Verde scowled.

"Did you ever hear the fox talk?" Freddie asked him.

"Forget the nonsense, little boy," the man said gruffly. "Just keep your hands off the fox. Children are not allowed to touch it. That is a rule in this house."

As Freddie looked surprised, M. Verde turned on his heel and strode out the front door.

"I don't remember Uncle Henri telling us any

rule like that," thought Freddie. Then he said the same thing out loud to the fox.

"I don't either," replied the animal in his strange, high voice.

"You're talking again!" cried Freddie excitedly. Now maybe he could prove it to the others!

Calling loudly, he dashed outside and around to the rear yard. A minute later he came racing back with his sisters and Louis behind him.

"It's no joke," said Freddie breathlessly. He turned to the fox. "Please, Monsieur Foxy, say something!"

Nan looked at her little brother's earnest face. She was really puzzled. "Freddie," she said, "you know he can't talk."

"Of course I can," said the fox. "I could tell you a secret, too."

CHAPTER V

SPLASHDOWN!

NAN and Flossie stared open-mouthed at the stuffed fox. They were too surprised to speak!

"I told you so!" cried Freddie. "He does talk! You heard him!" He pleaded with the fox, "Go ahead, Monsieur Foxy. Tell us your secret!"

"My secret," said the fox in his funny voice, "is for you to find out."

The four children tried to guess it. Nan wondered if there was a tape recorder hidden in the animal. "But that couldn't be," she told herself, "because it answered Freddie's questions. It's a puzzle, all right."

Flossie was inclined to be afraid of the stuffed fox. "He's spooky." She refused to touch him.

Freddie was braver. He stroked the soft fur. "Please tell us your secret," he begged.

There was no reply.

Freddie went on, "You ought to talk to Monsieur Verde or Monsieur Noir. They're interested in you." He told the others of finding M.

Verde examining the fur of the stuffed fox.

At this moment Bert walked into the hall.

"What's going on?" he asked. "Is this a meeting of some kind?"

"Yes," said Freddie. "A special one. The fox talks!"

Bert burst into laughter. "Boy, that's something! I told you he'd talk. Okay, Freddie, make him say something."

The little boy put several questions to the fox, but there was no response. Bert patted his brother on one shoulder. "Guess this critter's temperamental. Better luck next time."

Freddie told him about M. Verde.

"Why would he be so interested in this moth-eaten fox?" Bert asked.

"Remember, he can talk," Freddie reminded his brother.

"How long has the fox been here?" Nan asked.

Louis answered. "Uncle Henri found it in the cellar when he bought this place five years ago. It was an old tumbledown inn then. Nobody had lived in it for a long time."

"Louis," Freddie spoke up, "does your uncle have a rule that children can't touch that fox?"

"Of course not," said Louis. "Who told you that?" Freddie reported what M. Verde had said.

"Those two men act very strangely," said Nan, and the others agreed.

"There is no use to worry about them," said Louis. "Let's go swimming!"

The children hurried upstairs and put on their swimsuits. Taking caps, robes and towels, they followed Louis across the yard and past the stable. Single file, they walked down a narrow path through the cool woods. In a few minutes they came out on the shore of a large, sunny pond. A big tree grew on the bank which sloped down to the water.

"Oh-oh, look!" said Bert quietly. On the far side of the pond they could see the two men in a canoe.

"We won't bother them," said Nan. "They're far away."

Splashing and shouting, the children failed to notice that the canoe was drifting nearer. The men were talking together and did not seem to realize it either.

Once, as Nan came up from a dive, she was startled to find herself only a few feet from the canoe. She could hear the men talking.

"We'll try one more time," came M. Noir's voice. "If it doesn't work, we will have to do it some other way." As Nan swam off, she wondered what they were talking about.

Meanwhile, Louis had led the boys to the big tree. He pulled down a cluster of stout grape vines which grew among the branches.

"Watch!" he said.

Hanging onto the rough vines, the Canadian

boy backed up the slope and swung out over the pond.

"Splashdown!" he shouted and dropped into the water.

"That's great!" cried Freddie. "Let me try!"

In a few minutes the boys were having so much fun riding the vine, they did not notice that the men's canoe had come closer. Bert took a good running start, zoomed high over the pond and let go.

"No, no!" Nan cried. "You'll hit them!"

Too late Bert saw the canoe beneath him!

SPLASH! He struck the water inches from the craft. It rocked wildly and tipped over. Yelling, Verde and Noir fell into the water.

As Bert and the two men surfaced, the frightened children swam toward them. "Is anybody hurt?" cried Nan.

"I'm okay," said Bert. The men were spluttering angrily, treading water.

"Hold onto the canoe," said Bert. "We'll tow you in!"

The two men grabbed the overturned canoe, and the older twins swam to shore with it. The other children trailed after them. As Verde and Noir climbed out of the water, Bert tried to apologize. They ignored him and marched off into the woods, their clothes dripping.

"Wow! Were they mad!" said Freddie.

"They should have been watching where they were going," said Louis.

The men's canoe tipped over.

"So should I," replied Bert soberly.

The children beached the canoe, then gathered their belongings and returned to the house. When Flossie and Nan were dressed, they went downstairs. Lisette was coming from the kitchen with a basket.

"I am going to the baker for special bread," she said. "You want to come along?"

The girls said yes and followed her to the Leclercs' sedan. They drove about five miles beyond the village and pulled up before a roadside stand. An elderly woman with short, curly black hair was walking over to a round-topped brick oven mounted on a stone base. She was carrying a flat, long-handled wooden shovel. She waved cheerfully to them.

"We are just in time," said Lisette, as they got out of the car. "Madame Bell is going to take the bread out now."

The woman opened the iron door on the front of the oven and slid in the shovel. When she drew it out there were five crusty brown loaves on it.

"They smell just bee-yoo-ti-ful!" exclaimed Flossie.

The woman smiled and said something in French.

"She's going to give us a treat," said Lisette. "It might spoil our lunch, but it's something special you ought to try."

The three girls followed her to the stand

where she slid the loaves onto a long cutting board. With a sharp knife she cut three plump slices off one loaf and laid each on a plate.

Next she dipped a wooden spoon into a crock of soft butter and put gobs of it on the hot bread. As it melted, she poured maple syrup over each slice.

"Bon appétit!" said Madame Bell, beaming as she handed out plates and spoons.

"That means good appetite," said Lisette. *"Merci,"* she replied.

"Is that 'thank you'?" Flossie asked.

Lisette nodded and the Bobbseys chorused, *"Merci!"*

While eating, Lisette chatted with the baker in French. Suddenly the girl smiled. "Good news!" she said to the Bobbseys. "Madame Bell's sister will take Alphonse!"

The girl explained that she had mentioned trying to find a home for the dog. Mme. Bell had said her sister would like a dog and probably would be glad to have Alphonse.

"Oh, wonderful," said Nan. "Let's call her up right away."

"She has no phone," replied Lisette, "but Madame Bell says she will be home tomorrow. She lives in Baie St. Paul. Her name is Larue."

"Will she be nice to Alphonse?" asked Flossie anxiously.

"Oh, yes," said Lisette. "I have met her. She is a kind person and loves animals."

After buying four loaves of bread, the girls returned to the car. As they drove off, Mme. Bell smiled and waved her wooden spoon.

On the way home, Lisette stopped at a music store in the village to buy fiddle strings.

"I must teach Freddie," she said.

Driving back, Nan remembered the two men in the canoe. She told Lisette what had happened at the pond and both girls laughed.

"I wish I'd seen them," said Lisette. "I'll bet they were mad."

She and the twins wondered if Verde and Noir would show up for lunch, but the men did not appear.

"They went out in their car," said Uncle Henri.

During the meal, the girls announced they had found a home for the dog.

"I'd be glad to take Alphonse to Madame Larue tomorrow," offered Mrs. Bobbsey. "Baie St. Paul is one of the places I had planned to show you children." It was decided that Louis would go along too.

Not long after lunch an old car pulled up in front of the house, and a husky blond man in overalls got out. Uncle Henri led him back to the stable to haul out the trunk and fix the floor. The boys went to watch.

The girls and Mrs. Bobbsey took the costumes under the big tree to sew on them. Flossie stayed for a while, then wandered off to the stable.

The big blond man was down in the hole. Uncle Henri spoke to Louis in French.

"He wants me to get a rope from the cellar," said the boy to his friends. "But it's dark down there."

"Can't you turn on a light?" asked Freddie.

"There isn't any," replied Louis.

"I'll go with you," said Bert. He took the battery lantern from the wall hook. "Come on!"

Freddie stayed to watch the men, but Flossie skipped after Bert and Louis. When they entered the kitchen it was quiet and deserted.

"Papa is taking his nap," remarked Louis. He opened a door near the stove, revealing the dark cellar steps. Bert turned on the lantern and led the way to the bottom.

"The rope's right here under the stairs," said Louis. He tried to pick up the big coil. "It's heavy!"

"I'll help you," said Bert. "Here, Floss, hold this." He handed her the lantern.

As the boys reached for the rope, Flossie said, "Shh! I heard something."

The children stood still and listened. There was a slight rustling noise in a far corner of the cellar.

"Shine the light over there!" said Bert softly.

Flossie beamed it across. All three children gasped in fright.

Staring at them was a cruel-looking, one-eyed face!

CHAPTER VI

A MIDNIGHT NOISE

"IT'S Old One-Eye!" quavered Louis.

Flossie's hands were shaking so, she could hardly hold the lantern. Even Bert's heart was thumping as he stared at the frightening face in the beam of the light. Moments went by and he did not move or speak.

"Wait a minute," said Bert. "I think it's a mask." He moved closer. "Yes, it is." Bert took the mask from the wall hook, and the other two children heaved sighs of relief.

"This explains the one-eyed face you saw at the window, Louis," said Bert.

"Let's go outside," said Flossie fearfully. She had had enough of the dark cellar.

The three hurried upstairs, and the boys dashed across the yard to the stable with the coil of rope and the mask. Flossie followed but stopped at the tree where her mother and the girls were sewing. "We found Old One-Eye!" she exclaimed. "Come and see him!"

"This is the face we saw at the window," Uncle Henri said.

The four followed her into the stable. Uncle Henri was examining the mask in amazement.

Bert suggested that the person who had been trying to get in the house had worn it to scare off anybody who might see him. But how did he get into the cellar?

"We heard a noise in that corner before Flossie turned the light there," Louis reminded him. "I'll bet the intruder was putting the mask up just before we saw it."

Bert nodded. "He got into the cellar easily, because the kitchen was empty. But how did he get into the house? Did you see any strangers sneaking around the yard?" he asked the girls.

"No," said Nan. "And the front door is locked."

"The bad man might still be in the cellar," said Flossie shakily.

"We'd better check," Uncle Henri decided.

"I'll go with you," Bert offered and took the lantern from Flossie.

Bert, Uncle Henri and the carpenter went into the house. The others waited on the back porch. In a short time the three returned.

"No sign of anybody," Uncle Henri reported, "but I'd better call the police." He hurried off with the mask, and the other man went back to the stable.

"I wish I'd gone for the rope," said Freddie. "I like adventures."

"Then I have one for you," said Lisette. "It's time for your first fiddle lesson."

Freddie grinned. "That sounds like fun."

The two went into the house, and soon odd squawking sounds came drifting out.

"I guess I'll go for a walk," said Bert, covering his ears.

Flossie and Nan and their mother walked back to the tree to work on the costumes. Suddenly Alphonse yawned and walked over to Flossie. He flopped down again and put his head in her lap.

"He likes to be with us," she said.

Nan patted the dog's head. "Tomorrow we have to say good-by again, Alphonse."

"Maybe he could sleep in our room," suggested Flossie, " 'cause it's his last night. May he, Mommy, please?"

"It's all right with me if Madame Leclerc says yes," her mother replied.

Later that afternoon two policemen came and searched the house. No intruder was found. Taking the mask with them, the officers left.

At the supper table Flossie asked Lisette to speak to her mother about Alphonse. "We want him to sleep in our room."

Lisette consulted her mother in French and then told Flossie, "Maman says you may have him, but you must not let him out after everyone is in bed. He's sure to get into trouble," said Lisette. The girls promised.

"I wish we had a dog to stay with us," said Louis. "If there's an intruder hanging around this house we could use a special guard."

"There is nothing to be afraid of," Uncle Henri told him firmly. "You know the police searched thoroughly. They found no one."

"But he might get in again," said Louis.

"Don't worry, said Freddie with a grin. "I'll be our watchdog." He barked loudly, and the others laughed.

"I have an announcement to make," said Lisette. "Right after supper there will be a song practice in the parlor."

A little later the gay French tune was rippling out of the piano, and the children were singing the words they had learned. Then Freddie practiced on the fiddle again.

"You're getting better," said Bert with a twinkle in his eyes. "I can tell what you're playing now. It's 'Three Blind Mice.' "

Freddie grinned and went on playing.

"I'm practicing something for the party, too," said Flossie.

"What?" Freddie asked.

"It's a secret," she replied.

After the young twins had gone up to bed, Bert asked Uncle Henri what the police had said about the mask and the intruder.

"They do not understand it either," M. Valjean said. "Why should someone enter my house only to leave a false face hanging in my cellar!

Nothing has been stolen. My sister and I checked every article. It is a real mystery!"

For a while the older children puzzled over the problem. At last they went to bed.

Around midnight, Flossie woke up. "Nan," she whispered.

The older girl awoke. "What is it?"

"I want a drink of water. Will you go to the bathroom with me?"

"All right," said Nan, "but don't wake up Alphonse." The dog was snoring heavily on the floor beside the bed.

The girls put on their slippers and robes and padded down the dimly lit hall. After Flossie had her drink, they started back.

As Nan was about to open their door, she thought she heard a stair creak. Catching Flossie by one arm, she put a finger to her lips.

"Listen!" she whispered. They waited. There was not a sound.

"I guess I was imagining it," said Nan quietly. She opened the door. Instantly a furry body pushed past her into the hall.

"Alphonse! Come back!" exclaimed Flossie.

The animal trotted to the head of the stairs. He began whining.

"Come back here!" said Nan and grabbed for him.

Too late! Barking loudly, he bounded down into the dark lower hall. The next moment there was a frightened shout, a crash, and the house was filled with barking.

Doors flew open along the hall. Everyone dashed down the stairs. At the bottom, Bert threw the switch, flooding the lower hall with light.

Beside an overturned table M. Noir lay flat on the floor with Alphonse growling and barking over him. Near him was the fox, which M. Verde rushed to pick up.

In the confusion Bert and Uncle Henri pulled Alphonse away.

Uncle Henri spoke to M. Noir in French. The man looked dazed as he answered.

"He's not hurt," said Uncle Henri. "I guess he was sleepwalking again."

M. Verde spoke up angrily in French.

"He's had enough of us," Louis translated. "They're leaving first thing tomorrow for Quebec City."

Although Uncle Henri and the children apologized for the dog, the men walked upstairs without speaking.

In the morning when the Bobbseys came down to breakfast both men were in the front hall at the desk. Grimly they paid M. Valjean what they owed, picked up their bags and walked out. Watching from the door, the twins saw them get into their blue sedan and drive off.

"I can't say I'm sorry to see them go," said

Uncle Henri, then added sternly, "But Alphonse should not have knocked Monsieur Noir down. The dog has a very bad habit of jumping on people.

"I'm glad you children have found another home for him. I will call Madame Bell now for directions to her sister's house," he added. At breakfast he gave Mrs. Bobbsey the instructions, which he had written down.

Directly afterward the travelers went out to the station wagon with Alphonse. As soon as the door was opened, the dog leaped into the rear of the car. During the long drive he sat up and looked out the window.

After a while Bert exclaimed, "Up there!" On their left was a high, narrow waterfall dropping from a wooded cliff. "How'd you like to ride down that?"

"That's Montmorency Falls," said Louis grinning. A little later he pointed out a big, beautiful church in a small town. "That's the cathedral of St. Anne de Beaupré," he told them, "where people go to be healed."

Near noon they passed through wide fields. In the distance sparkled the blue waters of a bay.

"This is Baie St. Paul," said Mrs. Bobbsey. She handed Bert a piece of paper. "Please read me the directions to Madame Larue's house."

Bert did so, and soon his mother stopped at a white frame building near the waterfront. They got out and trooped up to the door with Alphonse at their heels. Bert rang the bell. A tall woman with gray hair appeared. She looked surprised at the group before her.

Louis greeted Mme. Larue in French, introduced everyone and explained why they had come. Mme. Larue's face broke into a smile. She wiped her hands on her flowered apron and opened the door wide.

"Come in," she said carefully. "I speak English—a little. Let me see the dog," she added eagerly.

Nan and Flossie led him forward.

"Here he is," said Flossie. "His name is Alphonse."

The smile vanished from Mme. Larue's face. She looked hard at the St. Bernard. "Did he once belong to Monsieur Durand?" she asked.

"Yes," Nan replied.

"Then I know this dog!" Mme. Larue exclaimed. She folded her arms firmly. "I will not take him—never!"

CHAPTER VII

THE GREEN SHADOW

FLOSSIE beamed. "I'm glad you don't want Alphonse!" she exclaimed. "Now we can keep him a little longer."

"You must know Monsieur Durand," said Nan to Mme. Larue.

"Yes," she said, nodding. "Come inside and tell me how you got his dog. Alphonse is too full of mischief for me—ruins things. I couldn't take him."

The callers followed her into a big, sunny room with a shiny linoleum floor. Long windows looked out on the sparkling bay. There were large comfortable chairs and Mme. Larue invited the guests to sit down. Then Louis explained in French how Alphonse had come to his uncle's house.

Mme. Larue shook her head sadly. "So he had to give up his dog."

"Do you know where Monsieur Durand is?" Bert asked eagerly.

"But no!" She turned to Louis and spoke in French.

The boy listened for a little while, then told the others what she had said. Mme. Larue had met M. Durand some months before in Quebec City, where he owned a jewelry store. She went to the shop several times and Alphonse was always there.

"Poor Monsieur Durand," she said. "He lost all his birds, too."

"Did he keep birds?" asked Freddie, surprised.

Mme. Larue smiled and spoke again to Louis in French.

"They were not live birds," he translated. "They were made of jewels. Monsieur Durand had a hundred of them—all colors. The red birds were rubies and the blue birds sapphires."

"They sound beautiful!" Nan exclaimed.

"Yes, but they were stolen," said Louis.

He explained that the robbery had taken place a few years before, when the jeweler had exhibited his collection in his shop.

"The jewelry was not insured for its full value. He lost a great amount of money. After that, his business became poor. Finally Monsieur Durand disappeared, owing everybody money."

"And they never caught the thief?" Bert asked.

"Oh, yes," said Louis. "Three were caught.

They had dressed up like policemen and walked into the shop, then walked out again with the gems.

"The men escaped in a car," Louis went on, "and got away from the police somewhere along the river. Several hours later they were picked up in a motorboat. But the loot was not on them. It has never been found."

"They must have hidden it during the time the police were looking for them," said Nan.

"Were they sent to prison?" asked Bert.

"Yes," said Louis, "but they should be coming out about now."

"I feel so sorry for Monsieur Durand," said Mrs. Bobbsey.

"Yes," Madame Larue agreed. "Monsieur Durand was a nice man. And he loved Alphonse very much."

"They must miss each other," said Freddie.

"If only we could find Monsieur Durand," said Nan, "we could give Alphonse back to him. That would be best for everybody."

"Is there anyone who might know where he is?" Bert asked.

"He has a niece in Quebec City," Mme. Larue replied. "She is a television actress. Her name is Michele Durand. Perhaps she would know."

"May we go and look for her, Mother?" Nan asked eagerly.

Mrs. Bobbsey nodded. "I planned to take you

children to Quebec City for several days, anyway. We can go there tomorrow."

"Louis, too!" exclaimed Freddie.

"And Lisette," said Nan.

"Of course, if their mother agrees," said Mrs. Bobbsey.

Louis grinned happily. "I can be your guide. I know the city very well. It is fun there."

The callers thanked Mme. Larue for her help.

"It was my pleasure," she said, and wished them luck in finding the missing man.

A few minutes later the Bobbsey party was on its way with Alphonse once more in the back of the station wagon.

"I'm hungry," said Freddie. "It must be near lunchtime."

"We'll stop right here," said Mrs. Bobbsey.

Just ahead was a log building with a red roof. A large sign said "Restaurant." They all ordered vegetable soup, crispy fried fish and potatoes.

"These fish are so little and tender you can eat the bones and all," Nan remarked.

"They're smelts," said her mother, and explained that lots of them were caught in the nearby bay.

Food was taken out to Alphonse. Then, after a run, he returned to the car, and the group headed homeward. For mile after mile they saw nothing but farmhouses and cattle.

Suddenly Freddie cried, "A giant cow!"

Some distance ahead was a huge cow made of wood. She had big blue eyes, and brown and white spots over her body. On one side were the words, *Le Fromage*.

"That means cheese," said Louis. "It's a farm where they make and sell it."

"We'll take some back to your mother," said Mrs. Bobbsey.

She drove through the gate and parked behind the cow. The children saw that part of one side of the wooden animal had been removed.

"It's hollow!" exclaimed Freddie. Next to the opening was a long ladder and they could see a workman climbing down it.

As the children and Mrs. Bobbsey got out of the car, a blond young man in denim overalls came out of a barn nearby. He called to them in French.

"He's inviting us into the barn to see the cheese," said Louis.

Leaving Alphonse in the station wagon, the Bobbsey group followed the man inside the big, dimly lit barn.

"Umm, it smells good," said Nan as the sharp tangy odor of the cheese came to them.

For a while the children followed their mother and the man, looking at the huge flat wheels of cheese. Some were white and others golden yellow. The farmer gave the visitors a small sample of each.

Soon the tour was over and the travelers returned to the car. Bert was carrying a large white paper parcel of cheese.

"Where are Freddie and Flossie?" asked Mrs. Bobbsey suddenly. The small twins were not in sight.

Mrs. Bobbsey called, but the children did not answer.

A search was made in the barn, but Freddie and Flossie were not there. Just as they came outside, they heard giggling above them.

"Here we are!" came Flossie's voice. The young twins were peering down from the side of the cow!

"Surprise!" called Freddie. "We fooled you!"

Bert noticed that the ladder was gone and grinned. "We have a surprise for you, too," he said. "You can't get down from that ledge you're standing on."

The small twins looked below at the side of the big wooden animal and saw what he meant.

"I guess we'll have to leave you there," called Nan, winking at her mother.

"You wouldn't do that," said Flossie.

"No," said her mother, laughing. "You're right."

In a few minutes Bert found a farmhand who brought the ladder back. He helped each child down.

Mrs. Bobbsey and the small twins thanked

"Here we are!" came Flossie's voice.

him. Minutes later they were on their way again and arrived at Uncle Henri's house in time for supper.

M. Valjean's face fell when he saw Alphonse galloping up the steps. While Bert explained the reason, Nan and her mother took their gift of cheese to the kitchen.

"Merci, merci!" exclaimed both the Leclercs.

Nan told Lisette about Alphonse and asked if she and Louis could go to Quebec City with the Bobbseys to find M. Durand. Her parents readily gave permission for their son and daughter to make the trip.

"Mother says she certainly hopes we succeed in finding the dog's owner. And also I can do some shopping for her in the city," Lisette translated.

Soon after supper the telephone rang and Louis answered.

"It's for Bert or Nan—a collect call from Quebec City. Will you take it?"

The twins exchanged surprised looks. "I bet it's Daddy," said Nan.

"But he's way up North," Freddie told her.

"Maybe he finished his business sooner than he expected," said Nan, "and he's on his way back."

She hurried to the phone and eagerly accepted the charge.

"Hello," she said hopefully as the others clustered about.

"Beware, Bobbsey twins!" said an odd, muffled voice. "Do not come to Quebec City or the Green Shadow will get you!"

"Who is this?" Nan demanded. At the same time she held the phone away from her ear so Bert could listen too.

"I am the Green Shadow!" said the caller very slowly.

The voice seemed familiar. Then the twins heard a stifled snicker. They exchanged knowing looks. It was Danny Rugg, their mean schoolmate from Lakeport, who was calling!

"Okay, Danny," said Bert. "You can't scare us. So don't bother to try again." He hung up.

Nan repeated what the caller had said.

"Who is he?" Louis asked.

"A pain in the neck," said Freddie. He explained that Danny was about Bert's age, and he liked to pick on smaller children. "He's always making touble for us."

Just then Mrs. Bobbsey came into the hall. Nan told her what happened.

"How does Danny know where we are?" Flossie asked.

"That's my fault," said her mother. "I met Mrs. Rugg in the market before we left. She had heard we were going to Canada and asked where we were staying, so I told her."

"Everybody knew Danny was coming to Quebec City," remarked Bert. "He was bragging about it for weeks."

"He said he was staying in the biggest hotel," said Freddie.

"So are we," his mother remarked.

"I hope we don't see him there," Flossie spoke up.

The Bobbsey children trooped outside for a walk. They returned at dusk to hear a merry melody coming from the parlor. Lisette was playing the piano.

"Do you want to practice your song?" she asked.

"Oh, yes," said Nan eagerly.

"I think we should make up a song about Alphonse," Flossie suggested.

"That's a good idea," said Freddie. "What tune should we use?"

" 'Three Blind Mice,' " said Flossie. "Then you can play the fiddle while we sing."

For a few minutes everybody thought. Then Nan said, "How about this?

"Poor Alphonse, poor Alphonse!
He's lost his master!
He's lost his master!
He's lost his master and needs a home!
He's lost his master and needs a home!
Poor Alphonse!"

"Let's try it," said Freddie.

He took the fiddle from the top of the piano and began to play. Between the uncertain notes of the squeaky violin and hearing his name, Alphonse came bounding into the room. He sat down, threw back his head and began to howl.

The music stopped abruptly. The dog stopped too and looked from one to another. Each time the singing started, he joined in with loud baying. The children doubled up with laughter and finally had to call off the music.

Because of the trip next day the children started for bed early. As they climbed the stairs, Uncle Henri was locking the front door.

"No intruder can get in now," he said cheerfully.

Next morning Freddie was awake before Bert. Too excited to sleep any longer, he dressed and went into the hall. Nan was coming out of her room, wearing a pink skirt and blouse.

"I think we're the first ones up," she said, and with her brother started downstairs.

Suddenly they stopped short. The front door was standing open!

The next moment Freddie cried out, "The fox! He's gone!"

CHAPTER VIII

THE SLIPPERY MAN

"SOMEONE broke into the house and stole the fox!" Nan cried out.

She and Freddie raced upstairs to waken the others. In a few minutes everyone was down in the hall in robes and slippers.

"One of the front door keys is gone!" exclaimed Uncle Henri. He was behind the desk, checking his big key ring.

"That explains why the front door was standing open," said Mrs. Bobbsey. "But who would steal the fox?"

"Monsieur Noir and Monsieur Verde!" said Bert. He reminded everyone of how interested the two men had been in the stuffed animal. "I don't think Noir was sleepwalking at all! He just faked that when we caught him trying to steal the fox."

"I'm sure Bert is right," said Nan. She told what she had overheard M. Noir say in the canoe. "He must have meant if the sleepwalking trick didn't work, they'd have to get the fox another way."

Uncle Henri nodded. "Yes, and the keys were hanging in plain sight. It would have been easy enough to slip one off the ring when no one was around."

"Another thing," said Mrs. Bobbsey. "After those two men came, you had no further trouble with people trying to get into the house."

"No wonder," said Louis. "They were already inside! Before that they used the mask."

"I guess the men decided to get rid of the mask," Bert remarked, "so one of them sneaked down cellar and hung it there."

Lisette had been quietly translating for her parents. Now M. Leclerc spoke up loudly, his mustache twitching excitedly.

"Papa says we must find out if anything else is missing," said Louis.

For the next fifteen minutes Uncle Henri and the Leclercs checked all their valuables. Nothing was gone except the fox.

"But why would they go to all this trouble to steal an old moth-eaten fox?" asked Louis, scratching his head.

"That's what I'd like to know," said Bert.

"It certainly is not valuable," Uncle Henri remarked. "All the same," he added, "I have grown quite attached to the creature. The house doesn't seem the same without him."

"Those men said they were going to Quebec

City," Nan remarked. "If that's true, we may spot them there."

"Don't worry, Uncle Henri," said Flossie, taking the stout man's hand. "We'll get *Moosir* Fox back for you. And we'll catch those mean old men, too."

"*Muss-yuh,* Flossie," said Nan and Bert together. "Monsieur."

Flossie blushed and tried again.

Uncle Henri patted her blond curls. "That's better," he said. "Just keep practicing." He went to telephone the police.

Afterward Bert suggested that the front door lock be changed. "If those men still have the key, they may come back and take something else."

"You're right," agreed M. Valjean. "I'll call the locksmith."

An hour later the travelers were on their way with the dog in the rear of the station wagon. He had been provided with a strong leather leash.

"Are you sure the hotel will let Alphonse in, Mother?" Nan asked.

"When I called for a reservation last evening, I inquired about it. The clerk said that Alphonse would be welcome, but of course he must not disturb the other guests."

"Let him stay with us girls," begged Flossie. "He'll behave."

Bert grinned. "You *hope.*"

Two hours later the station wagon passed several handsome stone houses on a wide avenue.

"We're coming into Quebec City now," said Lisette.

Soon the streets grew narrower. The buildings were closer together and small, with high sloping roofs.

"Oh, it's so quaint!" exclaimed Nan. "Like pictures of a French village."

"Quebec City is very old," said Lisette. "It was founded as a log fort by Samuel de Champlain in 1608."

"Look!" cried Flossie. She pointed to a great stone building on a hill. "It's a castle!"

"That's our hotel," said her mother. "Le Chateau Frontenac."

Freddie pointed up the street. "A horse and carriage!" he cried.

Coming toward them was an open two-wheeled carriage with facing seats. The driver sat on a high seat in front of the passengers.

As the horse trotted past briskly, Flossie imitated the sound of his hoofs. *"Clippety-clop, clippety-clop,"* she chanted.

"That carriage is called a *calèche,*" said Louis.

Flossie clapped her hands. "Oh, let's ride in one!"

"Later," her mother said.

In a few minutes Mrs. Bobbsey drove under a stone gateway into a courtyard and stopped before an arched entrance. They got out, and a young attendant took their bags. They followed him inside, while another man drove the station wagon away to a parking area.

Nan held tightly to Alphonse's leash as they crossed the big, beautiful lobby. While Mrs. Bobbsey registered, the children looked around at the rich furnishings. Here and there were large green plants in fancy pots.

"You'll have to be a very good doggie," said Flossie, patting the big furry head.

The next moment Mrs. Bobbsey signaled to the children. They rode up in an elevator and walked down a deeply carpeted hallway. The girls took the first room with the dog. The boys were in the next and Mrs. Bobbsey had her bags placed in the third.

"We'll have lunch in fifteen minutes," she said.

When the travelers went down to the lobby, they locked Alphonse in the room.

"Maybe the desk clerk could tell us where to find Monsieur Durand's daughter Michele," Nan suggested. "After all, she's an actress and probably well known."

The older twins stopped at the large desk in the lobby and asked the young man on duty.

"She lives in the city," he replied in excellent English, "but she is not listed in the telephone book. She will be filming in the Lower Town at eight o'clock tonight, though. You can find her there easily."

The twins thanked him and joined the others in the dining room. They told about Michele.

"What is the Lower Town, Lisette?" Bert asked.

She explained that Quebec is divided in two parts. "The Upper Town is where you are now. We are high on the ramparts above the river. Down below on a level with the river is the Lower Town."

After lunch Nan got her camera, then the group took a walking tour of the Upper Town. Finally they came to the high fortress and battlefield where Quebec's most important battle was fought in 1759.

"This is where General Wolfe of Great Britain defeated General Montcalm of France," said Lisette. "Afterward the British Empire controled all of Canada. France lost the part she had held."

"But you still speak French," said Freddie, puzzled.

"Oh, but yes," Lisette answered with a smile. "The land belongs to Great Britain, but the people of Quebec have remained French in their language and customs."

"That's nice," said Flossie, taking Lisette's hand. "I like to hear you say French words."

The little girl began to whisper some of them to herself as she skipped along the ramparts next to Lisette.

"Look at the old guns!" Bert exclaimed. A

row of ancient black cannons faced out across the wide river. Quickly Freddie climbed onto one and stood up.

"Stay there," said Nan. "I'll take your picture."

Suddenly Freddie pointed behind Nan to the fort. "Look quick!" he cried. "It's one of the bad men!"

The others turned just in time to see M. Verde disappear around the great gray fortress.

"Let's follow him!" cried Bert.

He dashed off around the side of the building with Nan at his heels. The man was not in sight. They searched for a while, but could not find him.

"At least we know he's in Quebec City," said Bert. "We'll keep our eyes open for him." But the children did not spot either of the two men the rest of the afternoon.

That evening as it was growing dark, they walked down the hill from their hotel to a small building on the edge of the ramparts. Inside was an elevator.

The Bobbseys and their friends followed the crowd inside, and soon the car went slowly down the steep hill. When it reached the bottom, the passengers stepped out into a narrow street.

Suddenly Nan gasped. "There's Monsieur Verde again!"

The suspected thief was a short distance ahead. Bert passed the word to the others, and

Bert and Nan dashed after the suspect.

they walked swiftly, keeping the man in sight.

They hurried past rows of tall, narrow houses with shops on the ground floor. Once the man glanced back. Then he went faster.

"I think he saw us," said Freddie.

Moments later they came out onto a broad street which bordered the waterfront. Straight ahead was a boat. People were crowding up the gangplank.

"That's the ferry to Levis," said Louis.

"Where is *Mawsir* Verde?" asked Flossie. "He's gone!"

"Probably he's in that crowd boarding the ferry," Nan guessed.

"We'll go, too!" said her mother.

As soon as they were aboard, Bert suggested that they stand near the gangplank in case the man tried to give them the slip by getting off again. In a few minutes the big ferry started. All the way across the wide river the children searched for M. Verde, but could not find him.

"Maybe he never got on," suggested Louis.

Bert agreed. "He's plenty slippery."

On the return trip, the children stood at the rail and looked up at Quebec City. It was dark now, and their hotel with its high turrets was sparkling with lights. Lower down was a tall tower with an illuminated clock.

"It's eight o'clock," said Lisette. "Michele will be in the Lower Town now."

When the ferry docked, the Bobbseys and

their friends could hear music coming from a side street. They followed the sound and saw a crowd of people. Towering above their heads were bright lights on stands and a camera on a long boom.

"Michele must be here!" Nan said, craning her neck to see.

"She's the one in the flowered dress," a bystander explained.

The children made their way to the front of the crowd. A tall, pretty woman in a flowered dress and hat was speaking in French. With her was a dark, handsome boy, holding an accordion. At one side stood a broad-shouldered man in shirt sleeves.

Michele ran over to the watchers and drew some boys and girls into a circle around her. The accordionist began to play and the children danced around Michele, singing with her. It was a song Lisette had taught the twins.

"I know that one!" cried Flossie.

With a laugh Michele pulled Flossie into the circle. Happily the little girl skipped around with the others, singing in French.

Suddenly a voice shouted, "I'm the Green Shadow!"

The next instant Flossie felt a hard push. She stumbled and fell! As the little girl hit the ground, several other children tripped over her and went down in a heap.

CHAPTER IX

BIG TROUBLE

THE music stopped and the man in shirt sleeves shouted an order. He hurried over, shaking his finger at Flossie.

Quickly Michele picked the child up and put an arm around her. She spoke quickly to the man in French.

Then she said to Flossie, "He is the director. I told him it was not your fault."

The little girl said, "We came to ask you a question, but I can't remember the person's name."

She was interrupted by the man, who clapped his hands and ordered everyone to form a circle again around the actress. The music started and the song was sung all the way through without interruption.

"That was good!" cried Michele. "Now it is over!"

As the actress hurried off, the crowd applauded.

"Don't let her get away!" Nan called to Flossie.

The little girl ran after her, followed by the other children. Michele darted into a nearby antique shop. As she opened the door, a bell over the top jangled.

The singer did not look back. She dashed straight through the store and into a rear room of the shop.

The children saw that it was a storage room. Against one wall was a long mirror with a heavy gold frame. On a table beside it lay tubes of make-up paint and boxes of powder.

Nan was about to speak when the young woman gave a sharp gasp. She looked quickly among the articles on the table, then stopped and searched the floor around it.

"Did you lose something?" Flossie asked.

Startled, Michele stood up. "Yes!" she cried. "My gold watch!" Her big dark eyes were full of tears. "It was a present from my grandfather."

Just then a voice behind them spoke quietly in French. The children turned to see a thin gray-haired woman. She gently pushed them aside and hurried to Michele's side. For a few moments she and the actress spoke together excitedly in French. Then the older one turned to the children and asked them a question. Louis translated.

"What do you want?"

"Tell her we must talk to Mademoiselle Durand about something," said Nan. "And introduce us."

"First we'll help Michele look for her watch," Bert offered.

The actress thanked the visitors. For a few minutes they all searched the room. Nan noticed that some of the powder had been spilled on the floor in front of the mirror. But there was no sign of the watch.

Very much upset, the actress went behind a screen in the corner to dress. The gray-haired woman introduced herself as Mme. Fontaine. Then she spoke in French, which Louis translated.

"The lady says she permitted Michele to use the rear of her shop tonight for a dressing room."

"Did she hear anyone else come in?" Nan asked.

After questioning Mme. Fontaine, Louis reported that she had been upstairs in her apartment, and had watched the filming of the television show from a window. Suddenly she had heard her shop bell ring and hurried down. No one was there.

"Was there no one in the back room either?" Nan asked.

"No," Louis replied. "She decided the person had only opened the door, then decided not to come in after all."

"But someone must have entered, because Michele's watch is gone," said Nan.

"Yes, but how did he leave?" Bert asked. "There is no back door and no windows. And the bell only rang once, so he couldn't have gone out the front way."

Mme. Fontaine was listening to them carefully. "I speak a little English," she said. "This is not the first mystery in my shop."

Slowly, she told them that some years before, her place had been a jewelry shop. There had been a series of thefts there and also in the fur shop next door. The thieves had been caught and sent to jail.

"No one could ever find out how they got in and out without being seen." She gave a great sigh. "Now the mystery is starting over again."

"We're detectives," said Freddie proudly. "Maybe we can help you."

Mme. Fontaine smiled. "What I need most is a good watchdog."

The children exchanged looks. "We might have just the dog for you," said Nan. She explained that they had hoped to find the owner and return the pup to him. "But if we can't, maybe you could have him," Nan finished.

Suddenly Nan remembered that the dog belonged to Michele's uncle! Now was her chance to talk to the young woman!

The children waited politely while the actress was dressing behind the screen. She called out in

French to Mme. Fontaine, who began to gather up the boxes of make-up paint and powder. Then she packed them in a small leather bag and tossed it over the screen.

Presently Michele hurried out, wearing a red dress and carrying a large black pocketbook. Hurriedly, she kissed Mme. Fontaine and blew the children a kiss. She smiled and dashed toward the front door.

"Wait! Please!" cried Nan, running after her.

By the time she reached the street, the actress had jumped into a small taxi and was gone.

All the children were disappointed. Mme. Fontaine said she was sorry. "Michele was late for her next appointment."

"How will we find her again?" Louis asked.

"She has not finished the film," was the reply. "For the next few days Michele will be working here and there in town as you saw her tonight. You will surely spot her again."

The children thanked Mme. Fontaine, who walked with them toward the door. The shop was crowded with old tables and chairs, lamps with beaded shades and small marble statues. Near the door was a tall stand with a huge white egg on top of it.

"What's that?" asked Freddie.

"An ostrich egg," said Mme. Fontaine. "People used to keep them for ornaments. Now you do not see them around much, so that one is very precious."

The children looked about curiously for a moment or two. Then, turning to go, Nan accidentally bumped the stand. As the shop owner cried out, the egg slid off.

"Catch it!" Flossie gasped.

Bert leaped forward and caught the egg just an inch from the floor. As he straightened up, Nan apologized, blushing furiously.

"No matter," said the shop owner faintly. She took the egg from Bert carefully. "I must put it in some safer place."

She walked over to a corner and laid it gently on a wooden tray on the floor.

"That's better," she said, as the children left.

"Where's Mommy?" asked Flossie, suddenly realizing the twins' mother had not been inside the shop with them.

Just then Mrs. Bobbsey hurried up to them. "I saw Monsieur Noir," she said quickly. "I tried to follow him, but he got away in the crowd."

She explained that during the making of the television film, she had spotted the man leaving the fur shop next to the antique store.

"Old Slippery escaped us again," Bert remarked. "Well, now that we know both men are here in the city, we're sure to spot them."

"Why don't we tell the police?" Louis asked.

"We know they're guilty," said Lisette, "because they ran away from us."

The shop owner cried out.

"But that is not proof that they stole the fox," Nan replied.

"I'd like to question the person who was taking care of the fur shop," said Bert, glancing next door. "But it looks closed."

"Yes," Lisette replied. "When we were watching the dancing I saw a man come out. He locked the door and went off."

On the way back to the hotel, the children told Mrs. Bobbsey what had happened in the antique shop.

"Poor Michele," said Flossie. "She felt so bad about her watch."

"It would be easy to suspect Monsieur Noir of taking it," Bert added, "only he was coming out of the wrong shop."

"Yes," said Freddie. "There must be another thief around."

"I'd like to know where Monsieur Verde disappeared to," said Lisette. "I was sure I saw him go into the crowd on the gangplank."

"He must have left the boat," Mrs. Bobbsey replied. "There are lots of old buildings on the waterfront. Maybe he ducked into one of those."

As the sightseers reached the elevator to the Upper Town, Freddie spotted a long stairway nearby. "I want to try the stairs sometime."

Lisette laughed. "You'll have plenty of chances to climb staircases. Quebec City has a number of them going from the Upper to the

Lower Town or from one street to another farther down."

"Maybe we'll see one when we take Alphonse for a walk tonight," said Freddie hopefully.

As they entered the hotel, angry voices rang through the lobby. Several bellmen were racing among the chairs.

"What are they doing?" exclaimed Mrs. Bobbsey. The next moment she gasped in horror.

"It's Alphonse!" cried Nan as a great furry body dashed past her.

With the bellmen chasing him, Alphonse raced straight toward a man sitting in a big chair.

"No, no, Alphonse!" Nan called.

But the dog leaped up on the man's lap, then on over the back of the chair. It toppled, spilling the man to the floor. Barking wildly and wagging his tail, Alphonse ran this way and that, over and under the furniture!

"He thinks it's a game!" Bert said, trying to tackle the pup.

The head bellman also made a lunge for the dog, who bounded aside and hit a tall plant.

CRASH! It fell over, and the pot shattered.

Yelping with fright, Alphonse headed for the door. Just then two women entered. Brushing past them, the St. Bernard darted out into the night.

"No, no! Come back!" Flossie screamed. All the children raced outside, but the dog was gone.

"He'll get lost!" said Nan.

"Or run over!" Freddie wailed.

Upset, the children returned to the lobby. The guest who had been knocked over was on his feet. Mrs. Bobbsey and Lisette were apologizing to him.

A tall gray-haired man in a dark suit strode toward the children. He was wearing a flower in his buttonhole. Their hearts sank when they saw his stern face.

"Oh dear," said Nan. "I'll bet he's the manager."

Just then the twins heard a snicker. They turned to see Danny Rugg looking over the top of a tall-backed chair.

He grinned. "Oh boy, are you in trouble!" he taunted them.

CHAPTER X

LOST AND FOUND

AS the hotel manager walked up to the children, Danny ran away. Mrs. Bobbsey came hurrying over.

"I will pay for whatever damage the dog did," she offered. "I'm dreadfully sorry."

"That is not necessary, madame," said the manager stiffly, "but the dog cannot come back into the hotel."

"But he hasn't any place to go," Flossie blurted.

"I am sorry," said the man firmly, "but we cannot take a chance on him again."

"How did he get out of our room?" Nan asked. "He was locked inside."

The manager explained that the maid said when she had come in to turn down the beds, a boy had coaxed Alphonse into the hall.

"Danny!" the Bobbseys exclaimed.

They looked around for the bully but could not find him. Finally they gave up and went to their rooms.

"Poor Alphonse is lost now," said Flossie, her lip quivering. "He won't have any place to sleep."

"I'm sure he'll find something," said Nan kindly, but she too was worried.

In the morning she called the desk and learned that the dog had not returned. As she hung up, there was a knock at the door. Flossie answered. Bert stood there.

"Bad news," he said. "Mother just stopped to tell me."

"What is it?" Lisette asked.

"Mrs. Rugg is not feeling well. She called Mother and asked if we would take Danny along with us today."

"After what he did?" Nan exclaimed. "I guess Mother had to say yes." Bert nodded gloomily.

"Danny always spoils our fun," Flossie sighed.

"Maybe he'll behave with your mother along," Lisette spoke up.

"I wouldn't count on it," said Nan. She told Bert that Alphonse had not returned.

"I think we should tell the police he's lost," said Bert. "They could help us find him."

The girls agreed.

In a few minutes all the children met Mrs. Bobbsey outside her room and went downstairs. Danny was seated in a big chair near the desk. He looked sulky.

"Hello, Danny," said Mrs. Bobbsey pleasantly, and the children called out, "Hi!" Flossie added, "You're a meanie. You made us lose our dog."

Danny scowled. "I don't know what you're talking about. And I don't want to go anywhere with you."

"You'll have a good time if you try," said Mrs. Bobbsey. Nan introduced Lisette and Louis. Danny did not speak to them.

After breakfast Mrs. Bobbsey suggested that they go to see the Diorama.

"What's that?" Flossie asked.

Her mother said it was a show in which there were little figures of soldiers, settlers and Indians.

"They act out the history of Quebec in front of miniature scenery."

"Oh boy, that sounds great," said Freddie, and Flossie wanted to go, too.

It was decided that Mrs. Bobbsey would take Freddie and Flossie, while the older twins and the Leclercs reported the lost dog to the municipal police in the City Hall.

"We'll meet here in the hotel for lunch at twelve o'clock," said Mrs. Bobbsey. "Danny," she added, "do you want to go to the show or to the police station?"

"Neither one," he replied.

Mrs. Bobbsey sighed. "Then you'd better come with us to the Diorama."

A short time later the older children hurried from the hotel and walked down the hill. They passed a big statue of Samuel Champlain and stepped on a wide boardwalk overlooking the Lower Town and the river.

For a few minutes they leaned on the iron railing of the terrace and glanced up and down the wide stream. As far as they could see there was sparkling water.

Louis pointed to the left and said, "Way out there the river empties into the ocean."

"And somewhere along the shore is Uncle Henri's house," Nan added.

Suddenly Bert straightened up. His eyes were snapping with excitement.

"I have an idea!" he said. "I've been trying to figure out why Verde and Noir would want to steal the fox. I think I know!"

"Tell us," said Nan eagerly.

"You remember the thieves who stole Monsieur Durand's jeweled birds and were later caught in a motorboat on the river?"

"But yes," said Louis. "What about them?"

"Suppose that before the police caught them, one of the thieves hid the jewels in a stuffed fox —maybe in the fur shop. And maybe it was sold and now they're hunting for the fox."

"You mean two of the jewel thieves are Noir and Verde!" exclaimed Nan. Bert nodded.

"I see!" said Lisette. "They heard about my

uncle's fox and thought that might be the one with the loot in it!"

"Exactly," said Bert. "It makes sense that way!"

"Let's tell the police right away," Louis suggested.

"Wait!" said his sister. "It's only a thought. We can't prove it."

"Maybe we can," Bert said.

"How?"

Bert suggested that they tell their story to the police and ask to see pictures in the "rogues' gallery" of jewel thieves.

"Of course!" Nan agreed. "We'll know right away if two of them are Noir and Verde."

Excited at the idea, the four hurried from the terrace. Louis led the way to the City Hall police headquarters. Lisette spoke in French to the officer at the front desk, and he ushered them into a private office. A tall, thin man with gray hair invited them to sit down.

Lisette introduced herself and the other three. Learning that the twins did not speak French, the chief switched to English.

"I am Captain Denis," he said. "Tell me your story."

Bert related the children's suspicion about Noir and Verde and the jewelry robbery and the theft of the fox.

"Very interesting," the captain said, his dark eyes looking keenly at the boy.

He picked up the phone and spoke quietly to someone. In a few minutes a young policeman entered and handed him a batch of photographs.

"Look these over," said the older man, giving them to Bert. "See if you can pick out your suspects."

With the girls and Louis peering over his shoulder, Bert began to examine the pictures. Quickly they picked out Noir and Verde.

"These are the men!" Bert exclaimed.

The chief's face broke into a smile. "You are right! Those are two of the jewel robbers. The third is still in prison. The real names of these two are Rostand and Lysée!"

Bert looked pleased as the officer congratulated him on his detective work.

"We've seen the men in Quebec City," said Nan, and told about spotting them the day before.

The officer seemed surprised. "I'll send a man down to check out the fur shop," he said.

Before leaving, the children reported the missing dog Alphonse.

"We'll keep an eye out for him," the officer promised.

The children were eager to tell their news to the other Bobbseys, so they decided to go to the Diorama. Louis knew the way, and they hastened along, keeping watch for Alphonse, Noir and Verde. As they neared the little museum

where the Diorama played, the doors opened
and a small crowd of people came out.

"There's Mother!" said Nan. She ran ahead
and caught up with Mrs. Bobbsey. The young
twins and Danny were behind her.

Excitedly Nan told what had happened at the
police station.

"Why, that's wonderful!" said Mrs. Bobbsey.
"I'm very proud of Bert—and of all of you!"

The young twins beamed at the story, but
Danny scowled. "You and your old mysteries!"
he said.

"How was the Diorama?" Louis asked.

"It was keen," said Freddie.

"It was terrible," Danny answered. With that
he turned on his heel and ran off.

"Come back here, Danny!" called Mrs. Bobbsey, but he sped on, turned a corner and was
gone. "Oh dear," she said, "we'll have to find
him."

"Can't we just lose him?" Freddie asked.

"No," said Mrs. Bobbsey. "I promised his
mother I'd take care of him."

"Maybe he went back to the hotel," Flossie
suggested.

The group headed in that direction. Drawing
near a big fountain outside the hotel, they saw a
crowd of people standing around it, pointing
and laughing.

"What's going on?" Freddie asked. Just then

Danny scowled. "You and your mysteries!" he said.

a man walked away and the children could see into the circle.

"Alphonse!" Nan exclaimed.

The dog was standing in the basin of the fountain, lapping up water thirstily. The twins and Louis raced over to him, and Bert collared him.

"Come out of there, Alphonse!" he ordered.

The big dog wagged his tail happily and jumped down.

"Alphonse!" cried Flossie, hugging him. "I'm so glad we found you!"

"But what are we going to do with him?" Lisette asked. "He's not allowed back in the hotel."

"Let's take him to Madame Fontaine in the Antique Shop," Nan suggested.

"Excellent idea," said her mother. "You children go with Lisette and do that. Louis, will you come with me to find Danny? I may need an interpreter."

Twenty minutes later the twins and Lisette opened the door of the Antique Shop. As the bell rang, the gray-haired owner came from the back. She smiled when she saw the children and the big dog.

Lisette explained in French that she could keep the dog until they found M. Durand. Mme. Fontaine beamed and patted the St. Bernard.

Louis said that Alphonse's rope leash was in the hotel and they would bring it down later.

Mme. Fontaine thanked the children and asked questions about the care of the dog. Meanwhile Alphonse wandered off among the antiques, sniffing here and there curiously. Suddenly Nan spotted him in the corner near the ostrich egg.

"Come here, Alphonse," she called, "and sit down!"

The dog looked at her and started to sit.

"No, no!" Nan cried. "Not on the egg!" But the next moment there was a loud CRACK! as the dog smashed the egg flat!

The children stood horror-stricken as Mme. Fontaine burst into angry French.

"We're so sorry," said Nan shakily. "Please forgive Alphonse. He didn't mean to do anything bad!"

"Out! Out!" cried Mme. Fontaine and pointed to the door.

Shame-faced, Nan and Lisette pulled Alphonse to his feet and hustled him out of the store.

Meanwhile the young twins said again that they were very sorry for what had happened, and Bert said, "Please—we'll pay for the egg."

"No, no!" said Mme. Fontaine. "Just keep that dog away from here!"

Outside, the little group looked at one another unhappily.

"Now what'll we do?" Flossie asked. "Nobody wants poor Alphonse."

Sadly Freddie glanced into the window of the fur shop. He gave a squeak of excitement. "In there! In there!"

The others turned to see several fur coats draped over display racks.

"What is it, Freddie?" asked Lisette, puzzled.

"In the corner of the window!" said Freddie. He pointed to a stuffed gray fox.

"It's our Monsieur Foxy!"

CHAPTER XI

THE SPY

LISETTE and the twins pressed close to the fur shop window and stared at the stuffed fox.

"Do you think it's the stolen one?" Nan asked Bert.

"I don't know," he replied. "We need a closer look. Let's go in and see if the man will let us examine it."

"Alphonse had better stay outside," said Nan.

The young twins waited on the widewalk with the dog, while the others went into the fur shop. A short, dark-haired man wearing steel-rimmed glasses came from behind a counter to wait on them. He spoke to them politely in French, and Lisette replied, introducing the children and herself.

"Ah, the twins are from the United States," he said quickly. "I lived in New York for a while and speak some English." He said his name was Auguste Levant. Although he had a heavy accent, the children could understand him.

Bert said the fox in the window looked very

much like one which belonged to Lisette's uncle. "May we have a closer look at it?"

M. Levant frowned. "You are saying I stole that animal?" he asked severely.

"No, sir," said Bert quickly. "It may not be the same fox."

"And if it is," said Nan, "that wouldn't mean you took it. Please don't think we meant that."

M. Levant studied the trio for a moment, then nodded.

"You look like nice children. There is no reason why you should not examine the fox." He stepped to the window, reached in and brought out the stuffed creature.

Nan and Bert looked it over. "This seems to be the same one," said Bert, "but I'm not certain. What do you say, Lisette?"

The teenager shook her head doubtfully. "To tell the truth, I never paid much attention to the fox, so I'm not sure. Louis could tell us, because he sometimes plays with it."

"You know," said M. Levant thoughtfully, "it's funny about that animal. I really never saw the fox before this morning." He explained that he had gone into a closet in the back room for some beaver skins and noticed a brown paper bag on the floor of the closet. "I didn't remember having seen it before, so I opened the bag and there was the fox. I thought my partner had put it there."

"Did you ask him?" Nan said.

"No. He's in South America on a vacation."

Bert inquired if a policeman had come to the shop yet.

"Yes. Early this morning," said the little man.

"Did he see the fox?" asked Nan.

"No. I did not find it until after he had gone. The creature has only been in the window about half an hour." He frowned. "How did you know about the officer?"

Lisette replied that one of the men suspected of stealing the fox had been seen leaving the fur shop late the afternoon before.

"I see," said M. Levant. "The police officer did not mention the theft of the fox. But he did ask if I recalled a thin, pale man coming in here yesterday."

"Did you see him?" Nan inquired.

The merchant shook his head. "Business was very slow, so I went to the basement for a while to check some fur shipments. The fellow could have come in and out then and I never would have known it."

M. Levant eyed the fox. "You think that man may have placed this in my closet?" The children nodded.

"But why would anyone steal an old stuffed fox and hide it here?"

The girls looked at Bert. He decided not to mention the jewels until they were sure this was the right fox.

"If this is the missing fox, the police can tell you all about it," the boy said politely.

"Yes, that's best," said M. Levant. "You come back this afternoon with your mother and the boy who can identify it." He smiled. "I get the idea that you children are detectives."

"We are," said Freddie proudly.

Nan asked, "Would you let us examine the closet where you found the fox?"

"Why not?" said M. Levant.

He led them through a door into the rear room of the store. Several dummies stood around with half-finished fur coats on them. Beyond was another door which Bert started to open.

"No, no," said the shopkeeper. "That goes to the cellar." He went to the other side of the room and opened a door. "This is the closet."

The children peered inside. Along the back wall were rows of shelves with pieces of fur lying on them.

"The bag with the fox in it was back in this corner," said M. Levant, pointing.

Bert examined the spot. Nearby he saw a crumpled piece of paper which he picked up. He opened it and looked puzzled.

"This is some kind of a note," he said.

Written in pencil were the numbers *8/6,* then 3 P.M. and the words *Queen I.* He showed it to the fur seller.

"This is some kind of a note," Bert said.

"I've never seen it before," M. Levant said.

"What can it mean?" Lisette asked.

"8/6 is August the sixth—that's today's date," Bert guessed.

"And 3 P.M. is plain enough," said Nan. "Something is going to happen today at three."

"But what does Queen One mean?" asked Lisette, puzzled. "Is it a place or a person?"

M. Levant shook his head. "I never heard of it before. You think the man dropped this note?"

"He might have," said Bert, and tucked the paper into his pocket.

As M. Levant was closing the door, Nan noticed splotches of light powder on the closet floor. Then the three thanked the merchant for his help and promised to return later.

Out on the sidewalk, they found the young twins waiting patiently with Alphonse. As they started back to the hotel Nan told them what she had discovered.

"Do you think M. Levant is in with the bad men?" Freddie asked.

"I don't believe so," said Nan. "He seemed very willing to help us."

Riding up in the elevator to the Upper Town, Flossie said she was hungry.

"It's nearly lunchtime," Lisette remarked, checking her watch. "But what are we going to do with Alphonse? He's not allowed inside the hotel."

The children thought over the problem. As they came out into the Upper Town, Nan said, "I know! Let's see if we can check him somewhere!"

The others thought this was a good idea, and they decided to try a hotel near theirs. They hurried up a hill to the big building and entered the lobby.

Lisette inquired at the checkroom if they might leave the dog and translated the answer.

"It will be all right, if he does not make any noise."

"Alphonse doesn't bark much," said Nan, "so I guess it's okay."

The checkroom girl opened a door beside the counter and took the dog in. She put a metal tag on his collar and gave Nan a disk with a matching number on it.

"Merci," said Nan.

"We'll be back for him later this afternoon," Lisette told the girl.

The children hurried to the Frontenac. Mrs. Bobbsey and Louis were waiting.

"Did you find Danny?" asked Freddie.

"Yes. In the Wax Museum," Louis replied. "We took him back to his mother."

"Is he coming with us again?" asked Flossie anxiously.

"Absolutely not," said her mother firmly. The children breathed sighs of relief.

Bert told his mother about finding the fox. As he was speaking, Nan happened to glance toward the arches at the hotel entrance. Peering around one of the stone pillars was a thin man with dark glasses and a full black beard. A hat with a wide brim was pulled down over his brow.

"Shh!" said Nan to Bert. "I think someone is listening."

As the others turned, the man slipped away into the hotel.

"He may not have been spying on us," said Mrs. Bobbsey, "but nevertheless we must be careful."

Bert finished his story quietly over the lunch table. Then Nan told about Alphonse.

"I don't know what we're going to do with him tonight," said Mrs. Bobbsey worriedly. "I'm sure they won't let him sleep in that checkroom."

"We must find Michele," said Bert. "Maybe she can tell us where Monsieur Durand is."

"Or she might take Alphonse herself," suggested Nan.

After lunch Lisette went off to do some errands for her mother. The others hastened to the fur shop, where Louis immediately identified the fox as his uncle's property.

"Then we must call the police at once," said Bert.

"Please, no!" exclaimed M. Levant. "An officer was here once today already, and I do not know what the neighbors must think. We are not so far from the headquarters. Let us take the fox there."

Seeing how alarmed he was, Mrs. Bobbsey agreed. The fox was put into the brown paper bag, which Bert took. They all left the shop together and M. Levant headed toward the elevator.

As they turned a corner onto a narrow street, Freddie let out a whoop. Before them was a huge fire truck with its ladder extended high in the air next to a house. A crowd of people was standing around it, blocking the street.

"Where's the fire?" Nan asked. "I don't see any smoke."

M. Levant asked someone in the crowd in French and nodded at the reply.

"There is no fire," he said. "Our streets are so narrow that every now and then the fire companies must practice turns in putting up the ladders."

"Oh it's keen!" exclaimed Freddie. He explained to Louis that he wanted to be a fireman when he grew up. "I have lots of toy engines," he said, "and my Daddy calls me his little fat fireman."

"And he calls me his fat fairy," said Flossie.

Just then someone bumped hard against Bert.

"Hey!" he cried out.

The next moment the bag containing the stuffed fox was snatched from his hands! Bert whirled to see the man with the dark glasses and black beard disappear into the crowd with the bag!

CHAPTER XII

THE QUEEN CLUE

"AFTER him!" cried Bert. "He stole the fox!"

The children pushed their way through the crowd trying to catch the man with the dark glasses and beard. He was gone!

Minutes later Mrs. Bobbsey, M. Levant and Lisette caught up to the twins and Louis.

Bert was furious. "We lost him and the fox, too!"

"He must have been following us," said Louis. "Probably he heard us talking in the hotel courtyard and knew we'd located the fox."

"Now what'll we do?" Flossie asked.

"I think we'd better report this to the police," said Nan.

Her mother and M. Levant agreed, so the downcast group headed for the elevator to the Upper Town. In ten minutes they were in Captain Denis's office. Mrs. Bobbsey told what had happened.

The officer shook his head. "Too bad! You

probably had the stolen jewels right in your hands!"

"I think the fellow in the dark glasses is Monsieur Noir," said Bert. "We didn't get a good look at him, but he's about the right size."

The captain declared that efforts would be doubled to locate the two men. Bert handed over the note he had found in the closet.

Captain Denis studied it. "Queen One," he said thoughtfully. "There are several restaurants in the city with the word Queen in the names. We'll check on them all at three o'clock. You children are good detectives," he added as the Bobbsey group rose to leave. "You mustn't give up."

"We won't," Nan promised.

When they were outside again, Bert snapped his fingers. "I forgot. I should have asked the captain if he knows where Michele is being filmed this afternoon."

"I can tell you that," said M. Levant. "It was in the paper." He gave directions to a stairway which led to a road below. With that he shook hands politely with all of them and said goodby.

They walked in the direction he had indicated. At the end of a street they saw the television cameras and a crowd of people clustered around them.

As the children raced up, they saw Michele.

She had on a black tuxedo suit with a high silk hat, and her face was painted like a clown's.

"Michele!" cried the young twins together.

With a merry wave the actress leaped onto a stair rail and zipped down out of sight! The crowd laughed and began to break up and move off.

"There she is!" cried Nan, pointing down the long, steep stairs.

The actress was standing on the street below beside a big camera. Around her were the film director and several other workers.

"Michele, wait for us!" called Nan.

She started down the stairs with the others at her heels. But Freddie hopped onto the banister and slid downward.

"I'll beat you!" the little boy shouted as he slipped past the others on the stairs. Faster and faster he went! Suddenly he knew he could not stop!

"Help!" he yelled. "Catch me!"

The next moment the little boy flew off at the end of the railing. He landed right in the arms of a husky cameraman!

Freddie was shaking as the man set him on his feet. Michele laughed and said, "That was a wild ride, little American cowboy!"

Moments later the rest of the party reached the street. Nan introduced Michele to her mother and said they were looking for M. Durand.

The actress leaped onto a
stair rail and zipped down.

The actress did not answer right away. "Lots of people are looking for my uncle," she said. "What do you want him for?"

"We don't intend to make trouble," Nan spoke up. "We would just like to give Alphonse back to him."

Louis explained how the dog had come to live with his family.

Michele chuckled. "I know Alphonse well."

"Perhaps you could keep him," said Nan hopefully.

Michele shook her head. "I would love to help you. But I live in an apartment where no dogs are allowed."

The children's faces fell.

"Then we must find *Moosir* Durand," said Flossie.

"I don't know where my uncle is," Michele replied, "but his sister may. She is Mother Angela in the Ursaline Convent here. You will need an appointment to see her."

Mrs. Bobbsey thanked the actress, who smiled and patted Flossie's soft curls. "I wish you good luck," she said.

The director called. Michele suddenly whipped off her high hat, made a deep bow to the visitors, and ran over to him.

"She's so nice," said Flossie with a sigh.

"Is it far to the convent?" Freddie asked as they climbed the long flight of stairs. "I'm tired."

Bert chuckled. "Too bad you can't fly up as fast as you went down."

"Why don't you children visit the Wax Museum while I make the appointment?" Mrs. Bobbsey suggested.

"What's in it?" Flossie asked.

"Figures of people made out of wax," Bert replied. "They're historical persons like kings and presidents."

"It shows them doing important things," said Louis, "like Columbus discovering America. It's a good place," he added. "I always go to it when we come here."

When the group reached the Wax Museum, Mrs. Bobbsey said she would meet them there in half an hour. Lisette went off to buy a sports dress, so Louis and the twins went into the museum alone.

While Bert bought tickets, the others looked at photographs of what was inside. Nan noticed that one of them showed Queen Isabella with Columbus.

"Look!" she said as Bert returned with the tickets. "Maybe this explains the note you found in the closet! The mark after the word Queen isn't a *one*, it's an *I*. It stands for Isabella!"

Bert's eyes sparkled with excitement. "You're right, I'll bet! The note is a reminder of a meeting—today at three o'clock at the Queen Isabella exhibit!"

Nan looked at her watch. "It's nearly three now!"

"Quick!" said Louis. "Upstairs! That's where the exhibit is."

He led the way through a red curtain at one side, and the children climbed a narrow, gloomy staircase into a dimly lit hall.

Along both sides were lighted glass cases. The children hurried past the colorful scenes, hardly stopping to look.

"Here we are!" said Nan softly.

Before them was the wax figure of the Spanish Queen in a beautiful wide-skirted gown. Columbus was showing her a round globe.

"They look so real," Flossie whispered.

"Everybody spread out," said Bert quietly. "Stand looking into the glass cases, but keep your eyes open for Noir and Verde."

As the others obeyed, he and Nan stood close together at the case next to the Columbus scene. Presently they saw the bearded man with dark glasses and a slouch hat approaching. From the other side, out of the shadows, came another man in the same disguise.

As the first man spoke quietly in French, Nan squeezed Bert's arm. He was M. Noir.

"Speak English," said the other man quickly. He was Verde. "How many times do I have to tell you? Not so many people here understand English."

"All right," grumbled Noir.

"Where is the fox now?"

"Down in the secret place," replied Noir. "I snatched it away from the Bobbsey boy."

"It's your fault he had the fox to begin with," said Verde angrily. "Why did you leave it in that closet?"

"I told you," said Noir. "I meant to put the fox down in our special spot, but as soon as I was in the closet I heard the fur man go down to the cellar. Naturally I couldn't go out that way. I was lucky to slip away through the shop."

"But why didn't you take the fox with you?" asked Verde crossly.

"I was afraid," said Noir. "Suppose someone had caught me with it!"

"You've lost your nerve," said Verde coldly. "Since we've been free you've taken only one piece of jewelry. I've lifted all the rest—fifteen rings and bracelets."

"It's too dangerous," said Noir. "Those Bobbsey twins are on our trail. They've gone to the police, I'm sure."

"Don't worry," said Verde smoothly. "In a day or two we'll pull the big job, pick up the fox and clear out. But first we'll go out to the mill." He chuckled. "It is a really fine hiding place."

"I hope we can find it again," said Noir.

"Idiot!" Verde muttered. "You just look for the little bridge!" As he spoke, the thief spotted Bert and Nan.

"The twins!" he hissed. "Run!"

Instantly the two men dashed down the hall.

"Catch them!" cried Bert as all the children raced after them.

The two thieves bounded up a narrow staircase to a top floor. They ran past the lighted windows there and turned a corner. Moments later the older twins and Freddie dashed around it after them. Across the hall was an open door.

"They went in there!" cried Freddie. The Bobbseys raced inside. The room was empty.

Bang! The door closed!

Whirling, Bert grabbed the handle as the key turned in the lock. "We've been tricked!" he cried.

CHAPTER XIII

BERT'S HUNCH

BERT and Nan pounded on the door while Freddie shouted for help.

"Unlock this door!" Nan ordered.

"I can't!" came Flossie's voice from outside the room. "The men took the key!"

"Are you all right?" Bert asked. "Where's Louis?"

"He ran after the men," said Flossie. "We're not hurt."

She explained that after the older children and Freddie dashed through the open doorway, the two thieves had locked the children in. "They pushed us aside and ran downstairs."

"Go get the manager, Floss," said Nan.

"All right," she replied.

Bert and Nan looked around. The room was a plainly furnished office. Bert stepped to a small window under the sloping roof.

"Do you see the men?" Nan asked him.

"I can't see the sidewalk from here," Bert replied.

In a few minutes there were footsteps in the hall and a tall, middle-aged man unlocked the door. Louis, Flossie and a policeman were with him.

The man looked serious and beckoned the children to follow him downstairs. On the way Louis reported that he had chased the men to the sidewalk and around the corner.

"They got in a blue car and drove off."

"Did you get the license number?" Bert asked.

"No. The plate was covered with mud. But I got the policeman."

With Louis as interpreter, the officer took a statement from the children and wrote it in a book. Then he spoke to Louis in French. The boy translated.

"He thinks the mill Noir mentioned might be their hideout. It could be on the Island of Orléans in the river. There are some old mills over there. The police will investigate them."

The officer closed his book, thanked the children and left. As they went outside, Mrs. Bobbsey arrived. Quickly the twins told her what had happened.

"It's too bad the men got away," she said. "Sounds as if they're planning another robbery."

"Yes, but maybe the police will be able to find their hideout and stop them," said Nan.

"I have good news for you from the convent,"

said Mrs. Bobbsey. "Mother Angela will see you in fifteen minutes. I have explained what you want. There is no need for all of us to go," she added, "and I have shopping to do. I will meet you in the hotel lobby in two hours."

Louis knew where the convent was and led the children a short distance to a large brick building behind an iron fence. He opened the front door and they entered a bare, well-scrubbed hall. It was very quiet.

"Where is everybody?" Flossie whispered.

"You'll see," said Louis. He walked over to a round, gold-colored grill on one wall. He spoke into it and a soft voice replied.

A minute later a door opened on the other side of the hall. A young, plump-faced nun beckoned the children inside.

They went into a simply furnished waiting room. At the window hung thin white and tan curtains. Modern chairs with bright blue or orange seats stood against the walls.

The young woman invited them to sit down. Then she disappeared. In a few minutes a middle-aged nun came in. She wore a flowing black-and-white habit and rimless glasses.

The Bobbseys and Louis stood up.

"I hear you are looking for my brother, Maurice Durand," she said.

"Yes, Reverend Mother," replied Louis.

She looked searchingly at each child. "He usually does not see people," she said.

"We want to give him back his dog," said Nan, "and we have important news for him." She told about Alphonse and their suspicions about the thieves of her brother's jewelry.

"They stole our fox that can talk," said Freddie, and the nun smiled.

"You seem to be very helpful children. Come with me," said Mother Angela.

The visitors followed her into a large garden. Suddenly she stopped and looked around.

"Is something the matter?" Nan asked.

"Yes," the nun replied. "I left my brother here and now he's gone! Perhaps I should not have told him that you children were coming."

"You mean he was right here and we missed him!" said Bert.

Mother Angela nodded. "Maurice happened to come here a few minutes before you arrived. I suggested that he should see you."

As the children stood in disappointment, Flossie noticed a man's white handkerchief caught on a nearby rosebush. She pulled it off carefully and saw the initials MD in the corner.

"*Moosoo* Durand must have come this way," she thought.

Her eyes wandered to a tall clump of bushes. Among the leaves at the bottom she spotted a pair of shoes.

Flossie clutched Bert's sleeve. "There he is!" she exclaimed. "*Moosoo* Durand," she called, "please come out!"

A thin, tired-looking man with gray hair stepped from behind the bush, his head down.

"Maurice," said Mother Angela, "these children have news for you."

"We want to tell you about Alphonse," added Bert.

At the mention of the dog, the man looked up. "What is the matter with him? Is he sick?" he asked anxiously. His English was very good.

"Come sit down," said Mother Angela.

She led them all into a white summerhouse at the end of the garden. There she told him the visitors' names. As Nan began to talk, the nun slipped away quietly.

When the story was over, M. Durand looked at the twins and Louis in amazement. "You are remarkable children!"

"The best part," said Bert, "is that Alphonse can go home with you now."

"I'm afraid not," said the man sadly. "You see I can hardly support myself these days. I could never feed Alphonse."

He explained that he felt very much ashamed and afraid because he could not pay what he owed people. "So I changed my name and I am working at a job to make money to pay it all back." He sighed. "But I'm afraid it will take a long time."

"When we find the men again," said Freddie, "you will have your jewels back."

"That would be wonderful," said M. Durand.

"These children have news for you," Mother Angela said.

"I would pay off my debts, buy back my store and have Alphonse again."

"The thieves are slippery, though," Bert said and told how Noir had disappeared at the waterfront.

"There are many places to hide down there," said M. Durand. "I've heard there used to be one or two old tunnels leading to houses in the Lower Town. In the olden days, when the city was besieged, people used them to escape by slipping away in boats at night. There were probably secret doors between some of those houses, too."

Mother Angela returned with a young nun all in white. She was carrying a tray with a pitcher of fruit juice on it and chocolate pastries.

"Please help yourselves," Mother Angela said, smiling. She explained that the sister in white had made the dessert.

The visitors bit into the delicious pastry.

"It's yummy!" exclaimed Flossie, and the young nun beamed.

"It is *Chiffon au chocolat,*" said the older nun.

The children repeated the name and thanked the nuns for the treat.

"Merci, merci," added M. Durand.

"I wish Alphonse could be here," said Flossie. "Chocolate is his favorite."

"And that reminds me," Bert remarked, "what are we going to do about him?"

"I have friends who will take him," said M. Durand. He pulled a pencil and a small pad from a pocket and wrote on it. "Here is the telephone number. The man's name is Jacques Bonnard. He's an artist and lives in Beauport. He and his wife have kept Alphonse for me before."

Bert thanked him. "And how can we get in touch with you, Monsieur Durand?"

The man started writing again. "I am going by the name of François Blum," he said. "Here is my address and telephone number." As he handed Bert the paper, he smiled. "I feel much better since I have talked with you children."

They all said good-by. As the children walked toward the hotel, Bert was thoughtful. "I wonder if there could be a tunnel from the fur shop to the waterfront," he said.

"Why?" asked Flossie.

"Because Noir said that the fox was hidden 'down in the secret place.' 'Down' could mean that it is underground. Also I have been wondering why Noir was in the fur shop with the fox. I'll bet he meant to hide him in the tunnel but never got that far."

"It makes sense," said Nan. "I remember that he said Monsieur Levant went to the cellar, so he could not go out that way. He could have been talking about going through the tunnel."

Bert glanced at his watch. "We have time to go to the fur shop right now. Let's ask Monsieur

Levant to let us examine his cellar for a secret entrance."

"We need flashlights," said Nan.

"I know where there's a souvenir shop," said Louis. "They sell little flashlights on key chains."

Eagerly the twins trooped off with him to a large store full of wood carvings, small paintings and toys. Bert bought five pencil flashlights with the words *Quebec City* on the side.

With the new lights in their pockets, the young detectives hurried to the Lower Town. Reaching Mr. Levant's shop, they stopped short. The shutters were closed over the windows. On the door blind was a sign printed in French.

"What does it say?" Bert asked.

" 'Closed for vacation—back in two weeks,' " said Louis.

CHAPTER XIV

FLOSSIE'S PICTURE

"WE'RE too late!" said Nan, turning away from the shop. "Mr. Levant left early."

"And he won't be back for two weeks," said Freddie. "We'll be on our way home by then."

"Now we can't search his cellar for the opening to the tunnel," Louis complained.

"Maybe we could find it from the waterfront end," said Bert. "We haven't time to go down there, though. It would take too long."

The disappointed children started back up the street. They noticed that the Antique Shop was shuttered. A sign on the door read the same as the one on the fur shop.

"Madame Fontaine must be on vacation, too," said Nan.

She thought of the night Michele's watch had been stolen. The thief could not have gone out the front door of the shop because the bell over it did not ring. How had he escaped?

"There must be a secret way out," she said to

herself. Instantly Nan remembered what M. Durand had told them about hidden doors.

"Listen, everybody," she said, stopping on a corner. "I have an idea. I'll bet there's a secret door between the two shops. The thief went out through the fur shop!" She reminded them of what the jeweler had said.

"Where do you think it is?" Bert asked.

"Behind the mirror. I'm pretty sure because I saw powder on the closet floor." She reminded the others that Michele's powder had been spilled on the floor in front of the mirror.

"You mean the bad man tracked the powder through the secret door into the closet?" said Flossie. Her sister nodded.

Bert grinned. "I'll bet it was Noir! Mother saw him come out of the fur shop, remember? And Verde said Noir had stolen one piece of jewelry. It must have been Michele's watch."

"But with the Antique Shop closed, we can't prove it," said Louis.

Bert agreed. "For the time being we're stuck."

The five started walking again.

"I wonder how Alphonse is getting along in that checkroom," said Freddie. "I hope he didn't sit on anybody's hat."

"We'd better get him out of there right after we meet Mother," Bert declared.

When the children reached the hotel, Mrs. Bobbsey was waiting in the lobby with Lisette.

Both were surrounded by bundles. They listened eagerly to the children's story.

Nan suggested that they return to Uncle Henri's house. "Tomorrow we can drive Alphonse to Monsieur Bonnard in Beauport. Then we can come back here and look for the tunnel."

"Good idea," said Mrs. Bobbsey. "Lisette and I will pack the bags. You and Louis go get Alphonse."

Half an hour later the Bobbseys and the Leclercs were heading out of Quebec City.

"Alphonse slept the whole time he was in the checkroom," Louis reported.

Several hours later they stopped for supper at a roadside restaurant. After a hearty meal, they bought meat loaf sandwiches for Alphonse, who wolfed them down.

It was dark by the time they reached M. Valjean's house. Uncle Henri and the older Leclercs welcomed them warmly. They were astounded to hear of the group's adventures.

"You have done very well," said Uncle Henri. "And now I will call Monsieur Bonnard. Tomorrow we say good-by to Alphonse again—for the last time, I hope."

The next day was Sunday. After attending church in the village, the Bobbseys had a delicious dinner prepared by M. Leclerc. There was pea soup with partridge in it, roast duck with oranges, and custard for dessert.

It was arranged that Lisette would drive the

children and Alphonse to Beauport in the station wagon. Mrs. Bobbsey would stay at home and help make party decorations.

"It looks like rain," said Lisette as they got ready to leave, so raincoats and boots were piled into the station wagon.

On the way the children practiced their French song and also the one about Alphonse.

"Now we'll have to change it," said Nan, "because he's found a home."

"Look!" cried Louis suddenly. "There's a mill!" Beside the road stood a red brick building with a big water wheel beside it.

"That can't be the one," said Bert, "because it's not hidden."

"There are a number of old mills up this way," Lisette remarked.

After a while they left the main road and went down a narrow twisting dirt lane in the woods. As they bounced over a small wooden bridge the children saw a creek not far below. Moments later they rounded a bend.

"That must be the house," said Lisette. Before them was a low, gray-shingled cottage.

A young man in blue jeans, with flowing blond hair and beard, strode toward them.

"Hello! *Bonjour!*" he said as Lisette parked the car. He called toward the house, "Diane!"

A tiny woman, also in blue jeans, ran out the door and came over to the visitors. Her black hair was tightly pulled back into a large bun.

Big dark eyes sparkled with friendliness. Both Bonnards petted Alphonse and laughed as he frisked around them.

"He remembers us," said Mme. Bonnard. She had a delightful accent. "And I remember what a wonderful sense of smell he has."

Lisette introduced herself and the children.

"Please call us Jacques and Diane," said Mrs. Bonnard. She invited them into the house, where a delicious aroma of cooking filled the air.

The living room was furnished with soft dark chairs and red curtains. At one end were paintings of the woods and the creek. Brushes and tubes of paint lay on a nearby table.

"These are Jacques' paintings," said Diane. "I'm an artist, too. I work in there." She invited them into a small studio with a drawing board in it. Beside a big mirror were several pairs of shoes and a pretty hat.

"I am a fashion artist," Diane said. "I draw pictures of clothes for newspapers and magazines. Now tell us about yourselves and Alphonse."

While the older twins told of their adventures with the dog, Flossie looked around Diane's studio. She could not resist touching the red plastic roses which covered the hat.

"I'll try it on," she thought. "If I'm careful I won't hurt the flowers."

She set the high, rounded hat on her head. It came down over her eyes! Flossie giggled at herself in the mirror. Then she noticed the dog sitting patiently beside her.

"Here, Alphonse," she said. "You try it on." She put the hat on his furry head. He rolled up his huge, sad eyes and woofed.

Flossie broke into peals of laughter. Freddie came in to see what was happening.

"Oh, Alphonse!" he exclaimed and began laughing too. This made his twin giggle all the harder.

The next moment Nan came to see what was going on. "Flossie!" she cried. "You know better than to touch other people's things without permission!"

"Wait a minute," said Diane quickly. She had come to the door with Jacques. "Don't scold her. That's such a funny picture, I must sketch it."

Flossie and Freddie had stopped laughing.

"I'm sorry, Diane," Flossie apologized.

"Never mind," said Jacques cheerfully. "Just put your arm around Alphonse and let my wife draw you!" Smiling shyly, Flossie did as she was told.

When the sketch was finished, Diane rolled up the sheet and gave it to Nan. "Take it home to your mother," she said.

"Now we'll have supper," Jacques announced. "Beef stew and fresh homemade bread!"

"I'll sketch you," said the artist.

"Oh, wonderful!" said Nan.

After everyone had finished, the girls helped Diane with the dishes.

"I hate to hurry you off," the artist said, "but we are going out this evening."

In a short time the visitors were ready to go. "Now we have to say good-by to Alphonse once more," said Louis.

With hugs and pats, the children parted from the dog. Alphonse whimpered and tried to follow, but Jacques put him inside the house. Lisette then tried to start the car, but the motor would not turn over.

"Oh-oh," said Bert. He and Jacques looked under the hood.

"It's the battery," Jacques said. "I'll have to charge it from mine."

While he moved his car up to the station wagon, the children got out again. It was growing dark, and a brisk wind was whipping through the trees.

Nan looked up at the heavy clouds. "I think we're going to have a storm."

Fifteen minutes later the battery was recharged. Once again the children thanked the young couple. As they drove off, Alphonse howled from inside the house. But he was drowned out by a clap of thunder.

In less than five minutes it was dark. Rain streamed down in sheets. Lisette steered carefully along the winding road. After a few feet she had to stop. The windshield wipers could not clear the glass fast enough.

"I'm scared," whispered Flossie as the thunder boomed and the lightening flashed.

"Don't worry," said Nan. "At least we're dry."

For half an hour the children sat in the dark road with the rain beating down and the wind howling through the trees. At last the downpour seemed to taper off.

"We'll try it now," said Lisette. She inched the car forward. Presently in the glare of the headlights she saw the little bridge they had crossed before. They moved slowly onto it.

CRACK! The station wagon lurched!

"The bridge is breaking!" cried Bert.

The next instant the car dropped into the creek!

CHAPTER XV

THE WHISPERING MEN

FOR a moment no one spoke. Then Lisette called out shakily, "Anyone hurt?"

"I don't think I am," said Nan. "How about the rest of you?"

"I'm okay," said Freddie.

Flossie was trembling, but she had not been hurt either.

"We're all right, I guess," said Bert, "but how will we ever get the car out of the creek?"

"I am afraid I've wrecked your station wagon," said Lisette. "I'm very sorry."

"It wasn't your fault," the Bobbseys said.

The children looked out at the darkness and the pouring rain. They could see one bank of the little creek in the headlights, and hear the water rushing around the wheels.

"One of us had better try to find a house with a telephone," said Lisette. "Our families may start to worry."

Bert opened the door on his side and leaned

out. He saw the water swirling close to the floor of the car.

"We'll all have to get out," he said. "The creek is rising."

After everyone had put on rain gear, Lisette told them to go straight up the bank in the direction the car had been headed. "No use turning back to Bonnards' house. They won't be home anyway," she said.

She took a flashlight from the car and stepped into the creek. The water came up to her boot tops. She and the older twins helped the younger children out, then they all started to scramble up the slippery slope to the road.

"Let's keep going to the village," said Lisette. "It's about a mile from here."

"Wait!" Freddie called out. "I see a light!" He pointed through the trees.

"Where?" chorused the others.

"I don't see anything," said Nan. "Are you sure?"

"I'm positive," Freddie insisted.

"Well, let's follow the creek and find out," said Bert. "If there's a house this close it's better than walking into the village."

Bert took out his little flashlight. The other twins and Louis turned theirs on too. With the beams lighting their way, they walked through the storm, water pouring off their hats. After a few minutes the creek widened and they saw a huge wooden wheel ahead.

"It's a mill!" exclaimed Bert.

Moments later they spotted a stone building amidst the trees beside the water. It was almost hidden among wild shrubs and was overgrown with vines. Part of the roof had collapsed and the door hung on one hinge.

"This place looks deserted," said Louis. "Are you sure you saw a light, Freddie?"

"I know I did," he replied.

As the Bobbseys stared at the old wreck, the same thought came to each of them.

Freddie remarked, "Maybe this is the mill where the bad men were coming."

"It could be," said Nan uneasily. "They mentioned a bridge."

"It's pretty far from Quebec City," Bert remarked.

"Maybe someone else took shelter from the storm," suggested Lisette. "Let's knock."

The travelers made their way through the high weeds to the door. Bert pounded on it.

"Anybody here?" he called.

There was no answer.

"Hel-lo—" called Louis and Freddie.

The mill stayed silent and dark.

Flossie slipped her hand into Nan's. "It's spooky," she whispered.

Just then lightning flashed. Thunder cracked and Freddie clapped both hands over his ears. The wind lashed the children's coats around them, and rain whipped their faces.

"We'd better step inside," said Bert. "When the storm lets up we can go for help."

He pushed the door wider and they all stepped into the darkness. A damp, sour smell came to their noses. In the beams of their lights they saw a large wooden chute which went up through a hole in the ceiling.

"The millstone must be on the second floor," said Bert. "When the grain was ground, the flour came down this chute in bags."

Here and there were rotting cotton sacks with the old flour spilling out of them. The children moved farther inside.

"Turn off your lights," said Lisette. "Save the batteries."

For what seemed a long time, the thunder rolled and the wind howled, so there was no use talking. Finally the storm died down. Bert was about to speak when they heard a loud creaking sound from the floor above.

Startled, the children listened. A man's voice said, "Don't be silly. They've gone."

Monsieur Verde!

"This *is* the hideout!" Louis whispered.

As Bert signaled for silence, M. Noir's voice came to them. "All the same, speak more softly."

Although the men began to whisper, their conversation traveled clearly down the flour chute.

"Those voices before sounded like the twins'," M. Noir said nervously.

"Nonsense!" snapped Verde. "They were picnickers who were caught in the storm. What would the Bobbseys be doing way out here?"

"They're everywhere, if you ask me," said Noir. "We know they've been following us. I think we ought to call off the special job."

"Noir," said his companion angrily, "you are what the Americans call a chicken."

"I don't care," said the other man stubbornly. "I say we should pick up the small stuff as soon as the rain stops. Then we ought to get the fox from the secret place and clear out."

"But we will never have such a good chance again to pull a double job with nobody around," replied Verde. "Think of it—two big hauls at one time."

"What if those kids get on to us and tip off the police?" asked Noir. "They heard us talking in the museum about the double job."

"Since they don't know where we intend to strike," said Verde, "we're perfectly safe."

Noir muttered a reply, but the voices became too soft for the children to hear.

"We must get the police as fast as we can," Bert murmured into Nan's ear. She nodded and passed the word along.

Silently, holding hands, the children picked their way toward the door. Suddenly in the darkness, Freddie stumbled over a flour bag. With a small cry he fell—*thump!* As the other children stood frozen, Nan and Lisette helped him quietly to his feet.

"I heard something," came Noir's voice from the floor above.

"Yes, I did too," said Verde softly. "We'll go down and check."

As swiftly as possible the children slipped out the door and ran toward the creek. The young twins and Louis were ahead with Lisette close behind. Bert and Nan paused to look back. There was no sign of the men.

"I wonder if they saw us," Nan whispered.

Bert did not reply. He had spotted an old round-topped oven standing on a brick base among the trees.

He whispered excitedly, "Maybe the thieves hid some of the stuff in there."

Quickly Bert pulled open the rusty iron door and shone his little light around. Inside lay a canvas bag!

Just then, in a flash of lightning, Nan saw two figures come out of the mill door.

"Run, Bert!" she exclaimed. "Here they come!"

Her brother snatched the bag and sped off behind her. They caught up to the others.

"The men are after us!" Bert told them. "Cut into the woods!"

"Try to stay together!" Nan warned.

"Run, Bert!" cried Nan. "They're after us!"

Each of the older three caught a younger child by the hand and they slipped in among the trees. After pushing through the wet brush for a while, they stopped to listen. The only sound they heard was the rushing of the flooded creek.

"Maybe they didn't see us after all," said Louis.

"Or perhaps they gave up," Bert added.

"Let's go back to the creek bank and follow it to the bridge," Lisette proposed. "We can walk down the road to the next village."

"Right," Bert agreed. "If we hurry we may be able to get the police before the men leave."

"But go quietly," Nan warned. "We can't be sure those men aren't still after us."

As the little group picked their way back toward the stream, Nan whispered, "Wait! I thought I heard something."

There was loud crashing in the underbrush ahead.

"It's the men!" cried Freddie.

"They've circled around!" exclaimed Bert. "Quick! Back into the woods!"

As he turned, a large dark body burst from the trees and leaped at him. With a cry Bert was knocked to the ground.

CHAPTER XVI

YOUNG DETECTIVES
AT WORK

AS Bert hit the muddy ground, a wet furry face rubbed against his cheek. There was a loud *Woof!*

"Alphonse!" Bert cried out, and the other children laughed in relief. "Get off me!"

Nan turned on her light. Grasping the big dog by the collar, she pulled him away from her twin.

"His rope is chewed through," said Flossie.

"How did he ever find us?" Freddie asked.

"Jacques said he had a remarkable sense of smell," Lisette reminded him.

"He must have really wanted to come with us," said Bert, getting to his feet.

"Noir and Verde might still be looking for us," said Louis anxiously. "We'd better get out of these woods."

He took Alphonse by the chewed-off rope and they started toward the rushing noise of the creek. Soon they were making their way along the bank. The rain had almost stopped.

"There's our car," said Bert. They could see the headlights of the station wagon under the broken bridge.

The next moment the children noticed lights of a car coming along the road.

"We must warn the driver that the bridge is out!" said Bert.

The children began to run up the embankment and shout at the approaching car. As they reached the road, Bert sprinted ahead.

"Stop!" he yelled, waving his arms wildly. The car slowed down and stopped.

"Bert!" called Mrs. Bobbsey from inside it.

"Mother!" cried the twins, who had run up.

M. Leclerc was at the wheel, with his wife and Mrs. Bobbsey in the rear seat.

"What happened?" Mrs. Bobbsey asked.

Quickly the story was told. Mrs. Bobbsey got out and looked down into the creek. She shook her head in dismay. "Thank goodness no one was hurt."

"Maybe we can find somebody in the village to pull the car out," said Bert. "Anyhow, we must hurry to the police and tell them about Noir and Verde."

"But first we ought to put a warning light of some kind on the bridge," said Nan.

When M. Leclerc understood her request, he took an electric lantern from his trunk. He clicked the switch and placed the lantern near the broken span. Then everyone piled into his sedan. The young twins sat on laps. Alphonse was squeezed in somehow.

"You're really sopping wet," said Mrs. Bobbsey. "And Alphonse is the wettest of all."

Fortunately the dog was wedged in too tightly to be able to shake.

In a short time they reached the village and pulled up before the small brick police station. A short, plump officer with heavy glasses named Ledoux listened carefully as Lisette and Louis told him in rapid French about the accident and the hideout of the thieves.

Bert handed over the canvas bag. When the officer opened it, he stared. Inside were fifteen diamond rings and bracelets plus a gold watch.

Nan picked up the watch. "Here's Michele Durand's name engraved on the back!" she said.

Lisette told Ledoux about the young detectives' activities in Quebec City trying to capture Noir and Verde. He looked admiringly at the children. Then he called in another officer and gave a long order in French.

"The village police will take cars and raid the mill at once," Louis translated. The chief picked up a telephone and made a call.

"He is telling the police in Quebec City," Lisette whispered, "that you have found this stolen jewelry."

When Ledoux hung up, he spoke to the Leclercs. Lisette translated.

"He says all of us should go to Quebec City tomorrow," Lisette translated. "The police there want to question us about tonight."

"Very well," said Mrs. Bobbsey. "But now we must get back to Uncle Henri's house at once. You children need hot showers."

After Ledoux had shaken hands with everyone and thanked the children, he promised to let them know what happened at the mill.

Louis added, "He also said he'd have the garage men raise your station wagon out of the creek in the morning," Louis told the Bobbseys. "They'll deliver it later to Uncle Henri's house."

When the crowded sedan reached home, the children took hot showers and put on pajamas and robes. They came down to the kitchen where hot cocoa and cupcakes were being served.

Presently the telephone rang. Uncle Henri went to answer it. When he came back, he said, "That was the police. They raided the mill. No one was there."

The children were disappointed and Bert said, "I was afraid of that. We were too slow."

Suddenly Nan remembered the artist and his wife. "Jacques and Diane will be worried about Alphonse," she said.

"I have already called them," said Uncle Henri. "They know he is safe. But they won't be home tomorrow, so we can't take him there."

"He'll have to stay here tomorrow, I guess," said Flossie.

"No, no!" Uncle Henri said firmly. "We are going to be very busy getting everything ready for the party. He will have to go with you."

"All right," Mrs. Bobbsey said. "I understand." But she sighed.

In the morning she drove the Leclerc sedan with the twins, Louis, Lisette and the dog crowded in around her. When they reached Quebec City, she parked near police headquarters. Taking the dog with them, the whole party entered and were ushered into the office of acting Chief Rand. He greeted them cordially, then listened with great interest as Bert and Nan told all that had happened the night before.

"You have done an excellent job locating the stolen jewelry," the chief said. "It is being sent to us by special messenger this morning."

"But we are still wondering where the fox is hidden," said Bert. "And what the double job is that the men are planning to pull."

"Yes, that is serious," Chief Rand said. "I doubt if they will go back to the mill again. The men must have discovered that the jewelry was gone from the oven and knew their hideout had been found. So they left. Think hard, children. Did they mention any other spot?"

"They talked about a secret place," said Nan, "but they didn't say where it was."

Bert told the officer his tunnel theory.

"We know about one tunnel," Chief Rand said, "but it has been bricked up."

Bert looked disappointed. "Do you know where it led?"

The officer shook his head. "No. I'm sorry."

Nan mentioned her idea about the secret door between the shops.

"That would explain how Noir got out of the Antique Shop with the watch," Rand said, "and also how the thieves who were caught years ago went in and out unseen, but it does not put us closer to Noir and Verde."

Chief Rand rose, thanked the children and ushered them out.

"Mommy," said Flossie when they were on the sidewalk again, "now may we go for a ride in a carriage?"

"All right," said Mrs. Bobbsey, "if Lisette will take you. I have some errands to do for her mother, and a few gifts to buy for home. I will see you in the lobby of the hotel—where we met last time."

Taking the dog, the children went to the big hotel where the carriages waited for customers. Bert and Louis boosted the big pup into one calèche. Freddie and Flossie climbed in and sat on either side of him with Lisette facing them.

Louis and the older twins took the next calèche. Soon both vehicles were bowling along beside the terrace of the Upper Town.

"It's fun!" cried Flossie. She waved at people and they waved back. Suddenly she cried out, "There's one of the bad men!"

She pointed toward the elevator. M. Noir in dark glasses and beard was just disappearing into the building.

Lisette asked the driver to stop and paid him. The children signaled to the calèche behind them. Flossie hopped down and ran back to explain.

The others paid their driver and the six hurried toward the elevator building with the dog. Impatiently they waited for the next car to leave. When they finally reached the Lower Town, the thief was not in sight.

"Maybe he's headed for the waterfront again," said Bert.

The young detectives walked along so fast that even Alphonse was panting by the time they reached the ferry slip. A boat was just sliding away from shore.

"Maybe he's on it," said Freddie.

"Yes," Bert agreed, "but he also could have ducked into one of these old buildings. Come on," he urged over his shoulder. "Let's explore up here."

They followed him into a narrow lane. Behind a large building which faced the water-

"It's fun!" cried Flossie.

front stood a low stone house with boarded-up windows.

The door was ajar. Cautiously Bert peeked inside. No one was in the shabby room.

Lisette and the children looked around at the heavy dust and broken glass on the floor. In one corner was a sagging sofa.

"It's just this one room," Louis remarked.

"Someone has been here," said Bert. "There are footprints, and see these long curved lines in the dust."

"These lines come from the sofa legs," said Nan. "It looks as if someone had slid one end of the sofa out from the wall and then shoved it back."

"Let's move it," Bert suggested.

The older twins pulled one end of the sofa forward.

Freddie gasped. "There's a big hole underneath!"

Excitedly Bert turned on his little flashlight. Sticking out of the hole was the top of a wooden ladder. The others crowded close and looked down.

"A tunnel!" said Nan softly.

CHAPTER XVII

THE SECRET DOOR

THE children were thrilled with their exciting discovery.

"You guessed it, Bert!" said Freddie. "This must be the tunnel to the fur shop!"

"We'd better tell the police," Louis advised.

"I think he's right," said Lisette. "For all we know, Monsieur Noir could be down in there now."

"But we're not certain that he went into this tunnel," said Nan.

"Anyway, this might not really lead anywhere," Bert argued. "It could be blocked off. Maybe we ought to explore it for a little distance first. If it looks worthwhile, we can send for the police."

The others agreed.

"What about Alphonse?" Louis asked. "We don't want him with us. He might make a noise."

They glanced at the dog, who sat watching curiously.

"Leave him here," Lisette suggested.

"One of us ought to stay in this room," said Bert, "to warn the others in the tunnel if the men should come."

"I'll stand guard," Lisette offered. "Be careful now," she added. "If there's any sign of trouble come right back or call for help."

The children promised and cautiously climbed backward down the wooden ladder. At the bottom they flashed their little lights around. Behind them, toward the waterfront, they saw a bricked-up opening. The stones around it glistened with dampness.

"That must have been the exit to the riverbank," said Bert quietly. "Closed up, just as the police said."

"But somebody dug an opening from above," whispered Nan.

Bert nodded and started along the tunnel away from the waterfront. After a few minutes he paused. The narrow passages stretched ahead, still open.

"I think we can take a chance that this leads to the fur shop," Bert said. He told the young twins and Louis to go back for the police.

"What about you?" Freddie asked.

"Nan and I will explore a little farther," said Bert. "Maybe we'll find the fox."

The younger children hastened away and the older twins walked on quietly. Rounding a bend, they saw that the tunnel ended at a wooden door.

"Be careful," whispered Nan. "There's no telling what's beyond."

Cautiously Bert took hold of the iron handle and pulled. The door moved outward with a creak.

The twins shone their lights into a small rock chamber. No one was there. In the center stood an old wooden table with a battery lantern on top. As Nan went to light it, Bert played his thin beams around the walls.

"There he is!" he whispered.

On a shelf stood the stuffed fox!

"We've found him!" Nan murmured happily.

Her hands were shaking with excitement as she turned up the lantern. As the little room glowed with light, Bert took the fox down and put it on the table. "Let's see if there are any jewels inside," he said.

"I think the opening must be around the neck," Nan guessed. "Monsieur Noir was feeling there when he pretended to be walking in his sleep."

Bert put down his light and felt in the animal's fur. At first he could find nothing but suddenly, on the back of the head, his fingers met something small, hard and flat.

"I think this is the head of a pin," he said.

With his fingernail he picked at it until finally the long pin came out. Bert was able to lift a flap of skin and reach inside. He pulled out a soft leather bag. Nan hardly breathed as he opened the drawstring and shook the sack over the table. Out spilled dozens of sparkling little birds.

"Oh, how beautiful!" she whispered.

For a few moments the twins examined the treasure, then Bert said, "We'd better get these out of here right away."

Quickly they put the jewels back into the bag and tucked it inside the fox. Nan fastened the flap with the pin. Her twin was looking up a wooden ladder in the corner. It led to the ceiling.

"Let's see where that goes," said Bert. "It will only take a minute."

He climbed up and found that a piece of wood covered a hole. It was heavy to lift, but Bert managed to move it aside. As he disappeared through the opening, Nan followed carrying the fox. The children found themselves in a neat basement with bales of fur stacked around. A wooden bin had been set over the opening.

"I was right," said Bert. "This is the fur shop."

"Yes, the tunnel led to it," said Nan. "Let's go upstairs," she added eagerly, "and see if we can find a secret door between the shops."

Quickly the children ascended the stairs and opened the door at the top. As they stepped into M. Levant's back room Nan gave a startled gasp. All the dummies were covered with sheets.

"They look like ghosts," said Bert softly.

The twins peered into the shop. A dim light filtered through the closed shutters. The showcase was bare.

"Everything is so quiet," Nan whispered. "It's spooky."

"I guess the Antique Shop is the same way," Bert remarked.

Suddenly Nan's eyes snapped with excitement. "Bert!" she exclaimed. "The double job the men were planning—they meant these two shops!"

"Of course! Nan, I see it now! They're going to rob both at the same time."

"It all fits!" said Nan. "No wonder Verde said they would never have such a good chance again. How could it be better? Both owners are away and the thieves can come in and out through the tunnel as they please!"

"I don't think they've been here yet," said Bert, "or they'd have taken the fox with them when they left."

Nan smiled. "We'll tell the police and they can be waiting here to surprise the thieves."

Bert grinned. "First we'd better be sure

you're right about the opening between the
shops."

The young detectives went into the closet. As
Nan shone her light over the back wall, Bert
pushed and pulled on the shelves. Nothing
moved. Then he took hold of a clothes hook on
the side and pulled. It turned downward! There
was a click, and part of the wall swung outward, shelves and all.

"We've found it!" Nan whispered. But the
next moment both children froze in fright. Before them stood the two thieves with a filled
burlap bag. For an instant no one moved.

Then Bert cried, "Run, Nan!"

The men dropped the bag and dashed
through the closet after the children. Down the
cellar stairs Bert pounded, with Nan behind
him hugging the fox.

At the opening in the floor, the twins scamp-
ered down the ladder. But Verde did not bother.
He dropped through the hole to the floor of the
secret room. Pushing the children aside, he
blocked the doorway. At the same moment Noir
came down the ladder behind them.

"We're trapped!" thought Nan, frightened.

"Hand over the fox," said Noir to Nan.

"I'll take care of it," Verde told him sharply.
"You go back and get the bag."

"There's no time," said Noir nervously. "Let's
tie the children up, grab the fox and get out of

"We're trapped!" thought Nan.

here. Somebody might come looking for them."

Bert and Nan knew they must keep the men talking until the police arrived.

"You won't get far," Nan spoke up, "because we told the police everything we learned about you."

M. Verde's eyes grew narrow. "What do you mean? What do you know?"

Speaking as slowly as she dared, Nan repeated all that the children had deduced about the men's actions beginning with the time they had hidden in the old inn.

"They know everything," whispered Noir furiously.

Bert spoke up. "We gave the police the stolen jewelry you hid in the oven at the mill."

"I told you so!" exclaimed Noir to Verde. "I knew I heard their voices."

His partner scowled at the twins. "How did you find the mill?"

"That was just luck," said Bert. Then he asked, "What made you pick such an out-of-the-way place?"

"When we got out of prison, we knew the police would be watching us, hoping we would lead them to the jewels. So we decided to wait." Verde said. "Finally we gave them the slip. Our buddy, who's still in prison, had hidden the jeweled birds in a stuffed fox in the shop."

"When the fox was sold," Noir spoke up, "we

had a wild chase finding it. Monsieur Valjean's proved to be the right one."

"Come on!" said Verde sharply. "We must get away from here!"

"Yes," Noir agreed. "Let's go!" He turned to Nan. "Hand over the fox."

"No," said Nan, and backed away.

Noir snatched the animal out of her arms and headed for the door.

"Drop me!" said the fox in his odd voice.

Noir stopped short and looked at the stuffed creature.

"Drop me at once!" the fox commanded.

With a yelp of fear, Noir dropped the animal. "It t-talked!" he stuttered.

"You idiot!" snapped Verde. "One of these children was talking for the fox—probably the boy. He must be a ventriloquist."

As Noir looked up he caught Bert smiling. Nan was so surprised she forgot to be frightened.

Verde's face was livid. "I'll teach you to play tricks!" he shouted angrily and started for Bert.

CHAPTER XVIII

CELEBRATION

AS Verde stepped angrily toward Bert there was a loud growl from the tunnel.

"Alphonse!" cried Nan.

At the same moment the dog leaped on Verde and knocked him forward into the room. Verde fell hard against Noir and both men crashed to the floor. Barking fiercely, the dog stood over the fallen men.

Nan snatched the fox and ran out the door. She and Bert raced through the tunnel.

The thieves scrambled free of the dog and dashed after the children. Alphonse bounded along last, barking loudly. At the tunnel exit Nan and Bert climbed quickly up the wooden ladder.

"Catch them!" yelled Noir.

Verde grabbed for Bert's leg, but just missed.

"Up the ladder—go!" cried Noir.

"I can't—the dog!" gasped Verde.

Bert glanced down to see Alphonse holding Verde back by his trouser leg. "That's right, Alphonse! Hold 'em!" he cried.

The older twins dashed out of the old stone house and into the narrow street. As they rounded the corner onto the waterfront they heard Freddie shout. "Nan, Bert! Here we are!"

The young twins were hurrying toward them with three policemen. Lisette and Louis followed.

"Come quick!" cried Nan.

Breathlessly she explained that the thieves were down in the tunnel. "Alphonse is holding them there," she finished.

Everyone dashed up the narrow street. As they crowded into the little stone house, they could hear the dog howling. The police flashed powerful beams into the hole. Alphonse was there all alone.

"Maybe the men ran back through the tunnel again," said Freddie.

A policeman jumped into the pit and headed up the passageway. Bert dropped down also and boosted the dog up the ladder. Then he came up again.

"I have a hunch those men didn't go back through the tunnel," he said. "It's too easy to get trapped there. I think they'll try to hide in one of these winding back streets."

Just then Alphonse gave a deep growl and headed for the door.

"Maybe he has picked up their trail!" said Nan.

The dog put his nose to the ground, then trotted out the door and down the cobblestone lane. After him went the twins, the two policemen, and Louis and Lisette. Except for them the street was deserted.

Suddenly Alphonse stopped by a high board fence and sniffed at a place where two planks were missing. Then he jumped through the opening and the others went after him.

"It's like playing follow-the-leader," thought Freddie.

Alphonse ran straight to two large trash cans beside the back door of a house. The dog gave a leap and knocked one can over. Out rolled Verde!

"So!" cried one policeman. Quickly he seized and handcuffed the man.

Meanwhile the children tipped over the other can and Noir fell out among a pile of old newspapers.

"Here's the other thief!" said Bert. Swiftly the second policeman handcuffed his prisoner.

Complaining bitterly in French, the men were led away, with the children and the dog at their heels. At the waterfront they were met by two police cars. The thieves were loaded into one and taken to headquarters. The children, Lisette and Alphonse followed in the other.

Nan hugged him. "Good dog," she said. "You saved the day."

Lisette explained that the younger children had been gone so long looking for the police she had decided to look for them.

"I left Alphonse on guard. I guess he felt lonesome, jumped down into the tunnel and went to find you."

When the car reached headquarters the twins and their friends were ushered into Chief Rand's office. The two thieves sat dejected on a bench, handcuffed together. Mrs. Bobbsey was there, too.

"Mother!" exclaimed the twins in surprise.

"Freddie told the police where to find me," she said and hugged all the children proudly.

"Madame," said the chief, "your twins are wonderful detectives!"

"Louis and Lisette helped, too," said Nan. "And Alphonse."

"Yes, and I thank you all," said Rand.

Blushing, Nan handed the fox to Bert, who opened it. Everyone gasped upon seeing the gems while Verde and Noir groaned.

"We will call Monsieur Durand," said the chief, "and return his property. Do you know where he is?"

Bert gave him the jeweler's address. "I'd like

"Madame," said the chief, "your twins are
wonderful detectives."

to ask these men a question, if it's all right," he added. The chief gave permission.

"Monsieur Verde, how did you learn about the tunnel?"

"From our pal in prison." The convict, it seemed, once had met an old man who told him about the entrance in the stone house. Years before, the old man had discovered a map which showed the opening in the floor, the tunnel and the secret door between the shops.

"We used the set-up to steal from the two shops," said Verde. "Our friend also told us about the mill."

After the men had been taken away, Bert and Nan related their adventure in the tunnel and the Antique Shop. Freddie and Flossie stared unbelieving at the part about the talking fox.

"Bert! You!" they cried, then burst into giggles. "You sure had me fooled," Freddie admitted.

Lisette and Louis laughed too. Then she said, "Bert, how about playing ventriloquist at our party?"

"What's a twillotwist, Lisette?" Flossie asked.

"Ven-tril-o-quist. That's a person who can throw his voice so it seems as if another person or a dummy is talking."

On the way home Nan said, "Let's invite Monsieur Durand and Michele to the party. We can give Alphonse back to him then." The others thought it a good idea.

When the Bobbseys and their friends reached the house, the station wagon was parked in the driveway. Uncle Henri met them at the front door.

"Your car had some minor damages," he reported, "but everything has been fixed. The garage will send a bill."

"Uncle Henri, wait until you hear our news!" cried Louis.

He called his parents and the full story was told. M. Valjean and the Leclercs were thrilled.

"I will phone Monsieur Durand at once!" M. Valjean said, and went off to give the invitation.

Meanwhile Flossie had run to the car for Diane's sketch of her and the dog.

Mrs. Bobbsey laughed when she saw it. "This is very good of you, dear," she said with a chuckle, "but tell Alphonse I like him better without a hat!"

The next day everyone was busy. Mrs. Bobbsey put the finishing touches on the costumes. Lisette and the children sang their songs and Freddie practiced his tune on the fiddle. Afterward they planned how to surprise M. Durand.

Later Nan found Flossie on the stairs whispering to herself. "I'm practicing," she explained to Nan. "It's a surprise, too."

In the afternoon delicious odors came out of the kitchen. Finally, at six o'clock, the children came downstairs in their costumes.

"You look wonderful!" said Mrs. Bobbsey.

Flossie had on a long dress with a print blouse and a shawl. Nan wore a full blue skirt with a white apron and many ruffled petticoats peeping out. The boys had on rough wool trousers and jackets.

"We're really old-fashioned!" said Lisette. She too wore a long full skirt with a bright apron.

The guests began to arrive and were greeted warmly by Uncle Henri. Last of all came M. Durand with Michele. The actress wore a ruffled yellow dress with a pretty hairbow to match.

"*Now,* Flossie," whispered Nan as the jeweler took off his hat.

The little girl picked up her skirt and ran upstairs. She opened the door of her room. "Come out, Alphonse," she said softly.

The big dog trotted to the top of the stairs. As he looked down, M. Durand glanced up.

"Alphonse!"

Barking joyously, the dog bounded down the steps and leaped into his master's arms. M. Durand staggered backward, but the older twins caught him. The man buried his face in the dog's fur. When he looked up his eyes were moist.

Before he could say anything, M. Leclerc bustled out of the kitchen. He wore a gleaming white apron and a high white chef's hat. Speaking loudly in French, he swept his arm toward the dining room.

Laughing and talking, the guests went in to the table which was loaded with delicious food. In the center stood the talking fox with a brown bow tied around his neck.

"How do you do," said the fox in his high, squeaky voice. "Help yourselves."

Everyone laughed, then took plates and filled them with food. They found places to sit down in the various rooms. The children and Lisette sat on the steps in the hall.

"We have to change Alphonse's song," Nan reminded them. They worked on it quietly for a few minutes.

"Now we must pass the cakes," said Lisette.

She and the children brought out trays of beautiful pastries M. Leclerc had made. Everyone praised the little chef, and his mustache twitched with pride.

When everyone had eaten enough, M. Valjean called all his guests into the parlor. There he gave a brief history of the old inn, then told how the twins had helped M. Durand and the police solve an old mystery.

"I have much to thank the Bobbseys for," the former jeweler spoke up. "I shall make each of them a little golden dog." The guests clapped loudly.

"Now we will have music!" announced M. Valjean first in French and again in English.

The twins and Louis gathered around Lisette at the piano and sang their French song. Nan then announced a special number.

Freddie picked up the fiddle and Lisette sounded a chord. The little boy played *Three Blind Mice* while the others sang:

Dear Alphonse, dear Alphonse!
He's found his master!
He's found his master!
He's found his master and has a home!
He's found his master and has a home!
Dear Alphonse!

Upon hearing his name, the dog jumped up and barked. As the guests laughed and applauded, Flossie said, "Alphonse wants to tell us he's happy again, but he can't talk."

"But I can talk," said the dog. "I'm very happy to be with my master again."

Flossie stepped forward and exclaimed, "Let me 'splain it!" She turned to Uncle Henri and said, "M'sieur Durand, and ladies and gentlemen, my brother is a ven-tril-o-quist."

Nan clapped her hands. "You said ventriloquist and M'sieur just right, Floss!"

Just then the fox called from the dining room,

"Open me! *I* have a surprise for the Bobbseys."

Flossie rushed in, pulled up the flap of fur and put a hand inside the stuffed animal. She brought out several little packages, marked with the names of the Bobbsey twins. As they opened pretty necklaces for the girls and penknives for the boys, Bert looked around to see who the other ventriloquist was.

Uncle Henri gave him a big wink.